Hair of the Dog

Lyle Hill

Copyright © 2019 Lyle Hill

ISBN: 978-0-244-51760-1

All rights reserved, including the right to reproduce this book, or portions thereof in any form. No part of this text may be reproduced, transmitted, downloaded, decompiled, reverse engineered, or stored, in any form or introduced into any information storage and retrieval system, in any form or by any means, whether electronic or mechanical without the express written permission of the author.

This is a work of fiction. Names and characters are the product of the author's imagination and any resemblance to actual persons, living or dead, is entirely coincidental.

Contents

Cesspit Baptism	...page 1
Larry Sparkle	...page 27
The Happy Boerboel	...page 33
Claw Hammer Romance	...page 44
Fresh Grotesque	...page 66
Baron of the Blue Bus	...page 92
The Old Man and the Lake	...page 106
The Firs	...page 125
Just Me and My Hunger	...page 147
Story from the Concrete Footings	...page 155
Fred (Under the Bed)	...page 174
The Chav Who Loved to Ride Horses	...page 185
The Christopher Hagen Jamboree	...page 196
Prophet of the Substation Wall	...page 205

For Matt

Cesspit Baptism

Dig it. I was cleaning vomit off my trainers when he knocked. They were covered in it – lumpy pieces of kebab that at some drunken stage I had devoured and then, at another drunken stage, spewed up on top of them. I had woken up on the living room floor. From there I'd dragged myself to the bedroom, stripped and collapsed. When I came to, I was dry-mouthed and bursting for a piss at the same time, so I went to the toilet and nearly fainted from the smell of my own urine. It was olive in colour and stunk like a rotting corpse. It was from the cheap, imported lager I had begun medicating myself on. It stunk like death. I even had to use the air freshener. *Air freshener for a piss?* I had never done that before.

After pissing I went back to the living room and sat down. I opened a lager and listened to *The Doors* while I cleaned my pumps.

It was a... *weekday?* I couldn't be sure.

If it was a weekday then I was fired. But I couldn't be arsed to check.

I was rubbing my Sambas with baby wipes when someone started knocking. I wasn't in the mood for human contact. None at all.

"WHOEVER THAT IS, FUCK OFF!"

Oh wait... I thought to myself. It could be the landlady. I owed her a month's rent.

"Mate, it's Joe!" Someone shouted from behind the door.

It was worse than the landlady. It was Joe. But wait a minute... "Who the fuck is Joe?"

"You know – *Joe!*"

"Joe *who?*"

"JOE!"

I pulled out my knife and undid the blade. It was six inches of lockable steel. It was a killer. I wasn't. But I was still drunk. And drunkenness could make anyone a killer. Not to mention I had been disturbed mid-trainer-clean.

I pulled the door open and saw Joe standing there. He looked scared.

"Why didn't you say it was you?" I hissed, pulling him inside and slamming the door shut.

He had vomit on his shoes too and started walking it into the carpet.

"What the fuck!" I shouted and started shoving him about in a panic, but this just spread the vomit around more.

He pulled them off. "Yeah sorry, some dickhead has thrown up outside your door."

"Yes... I, I know."

I lived on the sixth floor of Edward Gein House in Birmingham. It was a shit hole.

"So what do you want?" I asked him and sat back down with my lager.

"I'm right in the shit, mate. Right in it!"

I looked at him. Joe was a down-and-outer. He never had a job (as far as I could tell). Yet somehow he managed to keep the flat he had on the fourth floor. He was a weedy guy. Mid-twenties. Already balding. Childish face (with a childish brain to match). But I liked him. He was innocent and entertaining after a few drinks... (though he never bought his own).

"What's wrong?" I eventually asked.

"I've fucked up. I think I've killed someone."

This interested me. I finished the lager and tried to play it cool. "Go down the outdoor and grab a four pack." I held out a fiver for him. A fiver would be enough. I drank the cheap bollocks. And Joe drank whatever the fella buying drank.

"Did you hear me? Did you hear what I said?" Joe stuttered. He was desperate to take the fiver but still worried about his alleged murder.

"I'm not deaf. I'm thirsty. Go on..."

He took the money and left.

I'd fallen asleep on the couch and woke up to the sound of Joe letting himself back in. He looked nervous and I noticed one of the four pack was already missing and he seemed to be itching for a second.

"Give me a beer," I said and he did.

(Joe could dislocate every bone in his body. Some nights he did it to entertain us. One night I saw him dislocate his cheekbone. Another night, his hip. But I didn't think he would be doing any of that right now. He had killed someone, well, *maybe*.)

"So what happened?" I asked after the first glug. It was warm. They must have just been delivered.

"Do you know Kevin?"

"Why would I know Kevin?"

"He lives on the second floor."

"No."

"Big fat man. He has a ponytail and walks with a stick. He used to be a wrestler."

"No."

"Always drinking special brew?"

"Oh yes."

"You know him?"

"Yes, I've seen him vomiting before."

Joe thought for a moment. "Maybe he vomited outside your door?"

"Yes, maybe. So you killed Kevin then?"

"Well I was drinking at his flat. We were drinking special brew."

"Bad idea."

"I know. I know. Anyway, we started arguing…"

"What about?"

"Do you know Shannon?"

"No."

"She lives on the second floor as well."

"No."

"Skinny girl. Long, blond hair. Nice legs."

"No."

"Always smoking a spliff?"

"Oh yes."

"Well I shagged her the other night."

"Oh yeah?"

"Yeah. We were both stoned and it just happened."

"Well done."

"Thanks."

"But what does that have to do with Kevin?"

"I told him about it after a few special brews."

"And?"

"And he went berserk. He started swinging his cane about, saying he was going to kill me."

"So what happened?"

"Even with a cane the bloke could have battered me. He was twice my size. And in that small flat!"

"So what happened?"

"I stabbed him."

"Shit."

"I stabbed him with this knife."

Joe undid his tracksuit top and pulled out a tea towel. The towel was stained brown and folded inside was a pretty looking knife. It had an ivory handle and was silver plated. It was better than mine (although I'd never admit that to a scumbag like Joe). It too was covered in a strange brown fluid.

"What's that on it?" I asked about the brownness.

"I don't know. I think it's his blood."

"His blood wouldn't be brown, you cabbage!"

"He was pouring that when I stabbed him. Maybe he's ill?"

"I don't know," I sighed, becoming bored by the whole situation.

"Mate, you've got to help me!" Joe said, putting the knife away and rushing to sit beside me. He was too close. So I shuffled back.

"How can I help you?"

"We've got to hide the knife!"

"How will that help?"

"They need the murder weapon to prove I killed him."

"Did anyone see you go into Kevin's flat?"

"No. I bumped into him in the hallway. And none of the CCTV in Edward Gein's works. I just need to get rid of the knife. If Kevin's dead then the coppers will sweep the flats. They'll find it. I'll go to prison! I'll be raped!"

I glanced at Joe's balding head and his weird childish face. "No one will rape you, Joe."

"Will you help me hide it?"

"Okay."

"Oh man, you're a life saver!" He hugged me. "What shall we do?"

"I'm going to sleep..."

"But –,"

"Come back this evening."

Joe said he would and then he left the flat. I had two beers left and the kind of hangover that was more sedating than anything else. I was tired and my bones ached like flu. I had just agreed to help a moron cover up a murder. A few minutes earlier my biggest worries were cleaning my trainers.

"Bed," I said. Then I turned off *The Doors* and collapsed into the sheets again.

Maybe this would all be a dream...

Maybe I'd wake up fresh in a few hours and realise Joe had never visited.

I awoke totally *un-fresh* a few hours later and knew immediately that Joe *had* visited. I knew he had because I could hear him knocking again. Shit.

"Oh for god's sake," I grumbled, getting out of the sheets and staggering to the door.

I opened and saw Shannon stood there (not Joe). She was half-dressed and had the tail-end of a spliff hanging between her lips.

"Have you seen Joe?" She asked. (She did have nice legs.)

"No."

"I've been looking for him."

"I haven't seen him."

"He's not in his flat."

"I-haven't-seen-him."

"He came around to mine earlier. He was pretty smashed."

"Oh yeah?"

"Yeah. He said he'd been round here. He said you were his best friend and what a good bloke you were."

"Oh yeah?"

"Yeah… so you haven't seen him?"

"No. Maybe he went for a walk."

"Why would he go for a walk?" She stared suspiciously at me.

"He told me that… sometimes, he, sometimes he goes for walks."

There was a moment of silence.

"It's half two in the morning," Shannon said.

"He said he… he prefers walking in the dark," I was making no sense and lacking the energy to be creative. "Walking in the dark can be good…" Shannon looked at me uncomfortably and began to shuffle away. I watched her until she was out of sight. Joe was a lucky fucker.

Then I went back inside and started reading some Dostoyevsky. I had been trying to read *Crime and Punishment* for the better part of my life. I always failed. I liked the content of the book but I wasn't smart enough for it. So I laboured on, pretending I understood, pretending I was interested and letting the words go straight over my head – a swollen head – swollen at the thought that *I* was reading a Dostoyevsky (well... trying to).

Sometime later there was more knocking on the door and it was Shannon again.

"What do you want?" I asked angrily.

"I didn't want to come back but I still can't find Joe."

"Oh Jesus Christ, woman! He's a grown fucking man!" I shouted.

"He seemed upset when I last saw him."

"Of course he's upset – *he is Joe.*"

"What's that supposed to mean?" She glared at me.

"It means *if you were Joe* would you be happy about it?"

She stormed off (again). And I watched her from behind (again).

The night was becoming increasingly tedious and I was dying for a drink. So I pulled on some football boots from when I played years ago and left the flat in search of booze. I had no other footwear that weren't soiled in some way. Outside my door I stepped in the puke and screamed angrily. Several doors down the corridor moved as people peeked out or double checked their locks. I was not popular on my floor. I would get drunk and play loud psychedelic music or sleep in corridors or urinate or vomit in inappropriate places. *I* would not like me. In fact I did not like me. But I had no other choice...

(at least I wasn't Joe)

Then again, Joe had Shannon. Who did I have?

Dostoyevsky?

I suppose Dostoyevsky might as well have been a woman – he was complicated and I couldn't understand a fucking thing he said.

I was thinking too much. So I hurried down the corridor to the dirty lifts. They would take me to the ground floor, away from my sixth-floor-purgatory, and from there it was only a short walk to the all-night outdoor. If however, the outdoor was for some reason closed, then I was sure I would die.

The outdoor wasn't closed. I bought some lager from the Pakistani owner with the platinum teeth and then I returned home. The night was cold and cruel. When I reached the bottom of Edward Gein I saw Joe, perched like a weary pigeon and smoking a cigarette in the entry. The entry was usually full of urine-soaked tramps and, unluckily for him, Joe seemed to fit in quite well.

"Where have you been?" He asked when he saw me.

I gave him a can and tried to avoid his awkward glare.

"I popped out. Where *have you* been? Shannon keeps knocking on my door. She's spread vomit all over the hall with them heels she wears. Needless to say I'll get the blame for it. That Romanian family across the hall want any excuse to complain about me. They are bastards. Total fucking bastards!"

"I'm sorry. Look, I need to talk to you."

"Come up then."

Joe didn't talk on the lift ride up. He sipped at his beer with a shaky wrist. He was drinking out of fear – not out of the love of drinking. This was bad. I knew that. He was thinking drunkenness would build his courage and silence his worries but that never worked. Normally it made the worries worse and sent you insane – or you became foolhardy and made stupid decisions. I made a mental note to not give him anything else to drink.

In the flat he sat down and drained his can. Then he stared at the rest in my plastic bag.

"We need to get rid of this knife," he said.

"Yes, I know."

"Tonight."

"Okay."

"Where shall we hide it?"

"I've been thinking…" I opened a can for myself and sat down. I took the football boots off and saw Joe look at them, confused. "There's an old cesspit behind Edward Gein's. Have you seen it?"

"No."

"It's behind the substation."

"The what?"

"The electrics box."

"The what?"

"The box with electrics in."

"With what in?"

"Electrics."

"Electrics for what?"

"Oh Jesus Christ, just fucking shut up and let me finish! The electrics box, I mean, *substation* isn't important. But behind it is an old cesspit. We can lift the hatch up and throw the knife in. No one will look in there. They wouldn't want to."

"Will it be safe?"

"It will be submerged in waste. What kind of maniac would search in there?"

"The police."

"Have faith, Joe. Even the police wouldn't. Kevin isn't worth that much."

"Okay then."

So after I finished my can I put the stupid football boots back on and we took the lift downstairs. Joe had the knife in his pocket, still covered in brown sludge and wrapped in a tea towel. He said he had wiped his fingerprints off it, but I told him that wouldn't matter – no one would ever find it.

Outside I gave him a cigarette and lit one for myself. We walked around the back of Edward Gein's and to the old cesspit. It had a rusted-shut iron lid and on top of that was a whole heap of thistles and litter. Joe and I pulled the thistles back, cutting our hands and then we heaved the iron lid open. In the dead of night it was impossible to see into the old, out-of-use cesspit but the smell was bad enough. It reminded me of my super-strength-piss from the other day, only worse.

"Go on then," I said to Joe.

He carefully took the knife from his pocket and waggled the tea towel over the seemingly bottomless cesspit. But the knife was caught.

"Oh for fuck's sake," I reached out and pulled it free. Then I dropped the beautiful ivory blade into the darkness...

Out of sight we both heard it splash into the Victorian waste.

I slammed the iron lid back down and stamped it shut with my football boots. Then I pulled some thistles back on top of it. It was four in the morning. No one had seen a thing.

"I don't know how to thank you," Joe said and shook my hand.

"Forget it," I said and began back to the flats.

Back home I locked the door, drank beer and listened to *The Door's* final album *L.A. Woman*. At the conclusion of the final song I shed a single tear. Maybe for Kevin. Maybe for Jim Morrison. Maybe for my own shitty existence.

"Maybe I should have thrown myself into that fucking cesspit?"

The next morning I woke up early and fresh. I finished a short story I had been mutilating for the past few days and decided to post it to a publisher I admired. When I walked downstairs, I passed by Kevin in the lobby.

Wait – what?

I turned and looked. Wasn't he supposed to be…?

It was definitely him. He was fat. He walked with a cane. He had that greasy ponytail that looked like a dildo sticking out the back of his head. And he already, at half past seven, had a can of special brew in his hand.

"Didn't Joe –,"

I almost asked Kevin if he had been murdered or not. But luckily he didn't hear me.

So instead I continued outside, posted my story and returned to the flat. I had two missed calls from Joe, so I called him back.

"Hello Joe."

"Mate, how're you?"

"I just saw a ghost."

"Fuck! You saw him?"

"Yeah, what the fuck is going on?"

"Turns out I didn't kill him."

"So what's going on?"

"Remember I told you how he went mad after I mentioned shagging Shannon?"

"Yes."

"Shannon is his daughter."

"Right."

"She told me last night. She'd been looking for me. She was all upset because he was in hospital."

"Right."

"Turns out I stabbed him in his colostomy bag."

I pause for a moment. "So that was his shit on the knife?"

"Yeah. Cool, isn't it?"

"Not really, Joe. Not at all."

"Anyway he was so twisted on special brew he can't remember who stabbed him."

"Convenient."

"Yeah, right? I'm a lucky cunt."

I thought about Shannon's legs, "Yes you are."

"Anyway Shannon's hit the roof. Her and Kevin are on the warpath trying to figure out who it was that wrecked his bag."

"Why?"

"I suppose they find it upsetting."

"Anyway Joe, I've got to go."

"Okay, mate. Bye."

"Right."

I hung up and considered the whole situation for a moment. But then it became annoying so I stopped. I opened a beer and wondered how long it would take for the publishers to get back in touch with the good news. (Probably *a very long time...*)

I opened Crime and Punishment.

That evening I started another story. It was about a disfigured ice-cream man who sold frozen road kill. He collected the carcases of cats or foxes or partridges, blended them, added sweet sorbets, froze them and sold them to unsuspecting children. The words flew out with ease. It was a beautiful story. He fell in love with a woman who had been a tree surgeon. One day a silver birch crushed both her legs, so he sold her legs to the children and they all contracted hepatitis. The disfigured ice-cream man and the paraplegic tree surgeon woman went on the run and never returned. The final passage was about them driving down the M6, eating part of her calf and singing along to the radio. I cried.

"Perfection!" I said as I finished. I wrote a brief covering letter, describing my inspiration and quoting Dostoyevsky and *The Doors*, and then I sealed it to post later.

And then, once again, there was a knock on my door...

"Unless you're Fyodor Dostoyevsky, PISS OFF!" I screamed.

Then someone kicked it. I saw the weak, timber shake. My blood, like morning grease in a pan, began to sizzle in my veins. I rushed to the door, clenched my fist and pulled it open.

Shannon was stood there. Kevin was beside her. They both looked angry.

"What do you two want?"

"I've spent two hours trying to calm my dad down!" Shannon started. "He was going to come up here and kick your fucking head in!"

"What? You two are insane," I tried to close the door but Kevin jammed his stick in.

"Take that stick out! OUT!" I demanded. "Or I'll stuff it down your arsehole!"

"LISTEN!" Shannon shouted. "We know it was you. You got my dad drunk and then you stabbed his bag. Do you know how much a replacement bag costs?"

"Probably not a lot."

"WELL YOU ARE WRONG!"

"Listen bitch, you're round the fucking bend. It wasn't me who stabbed your dad's colostomy bag!" As I finished speaking the Romanian family opened their door and began to watch.

"JOE TOLD ME SO!" She shouted back. I paused. Surely not? Joe... *told her I did it?* I could feel murderous adrenaline building in my bloodstream. Something bad was going to happen, soon, very soon... "He told me it was you," she stated clearly.

"Joe is a fucking liar!" I hissed.

Kevin lunged for me, but Shannon stopped him.

"We just wanted to tell you," she smirked. "The police know what you did. They know where you hid the knife. They're on their way and when they find it you'll be going to prison."

I slammed the door on their ugly faces. Then I ran across to my phone and called Joe. It went straight to voicemail. I tried again. Same thing. Fuck it! I tore out of the flat like a hurricane wind. Sod the lift! I went down the stairs, jumping between the stair cases and getting down to the fourth floor in a record-breaking time. I was knackered – breathing so hard that my lungs were burning – but I was sure that I still had enough energy to beat Joe to death for his betrayal.

"JOE!" I screamed and banged on his door. "JOE!"

I saw a shadow fall over the peep-hole.

"I CAN SEE YOUR SHADOW, YOU CUNT!"

"Mate, I'm… I'm…"

"WHY DID YOU DO IT? WHY?"

"I…"

"TELL ME YOU LITTLE SHITE!"

"Last night I was with Shannon."

"AAAANNNNDDDD?"

"She wouldn't, you know… *give me any.* She was too upset about her dad. She was too angry that someone had done it to him."

"SO FUCKING WHAT?"

"I needed to drop someone in it… so she'd, you know, *give me some.*"

"NO I DON'T FUCKING KNOW!"

I started punching and kicking at the door, but it wouldn't cave in. I wanted it to. Then I'd cave Joe's fucking head in. I would smear his stupid childish fucking brains all over his linoleum floor. That bastard! That stupid, stupid bastard!

"I was stoned. I'm sorry. You'll have to get the knife back."

"What? From the fucking cesspit? Are you insane?"

"Shannon told the coppers where it was. They'll find it."

"You think I give a shit?"

"You should do – your fingerprints are on it."

"But... so are yours!"

"Nope. I wiped mine off. You threw it in. It's got your prints. And it's mine and Shannon's word against yours."

"I'll get you for this, Joe!" I said, beginning to creep away. "You bet I will. You snivelling little rat!"

He didn't respond and I didn't have time to curse anymore.

The more I thought about it I was digging a deeper hole by shouting and threatening to kill him in the hallway. The coppers wouldn't have to ask around much. Soon they'd get the vibe I was quite capable of slashing a former wrestler's shitbag.

Outside I walked slowly and depressed across to the cesspit. I prayed that somehow it had vanished or that the police had already found it and I could just go to jail. But neither had happened. As I walked behind the substation I looked down on the rusty iron lid and could smell the dank, heavy stench of stale waste... ancient, stale waste.

I heaved the lid open and felt the sour smell hit me at the back of the throat. It clung there. It was like nicotine stains growing on a pub ceiling. I could almost feel it solidifying and begin to drip and ooze down the back of my throat.

Below me was darkness. It truly looked and smelt like a passage to hell.

I didn't know how far the drop was. I didn't know how deep it was. All I knew was that the knife was down there and that without it, I would be going to jail.

I took a deep breath.

And then another.

And then, in the grips of insanity, I jumped.

The black didn't last long. I cut through it just like the knife I was looking for. And in one barbaric second I felt my body engulfed by a thick, gloopy liquid to the chin.

I had to tread to stop sinking. It was thicker than water and easier to float in. But it was lumpy and I felt myself vomiting. The smell of old waste ran up my nostrils like a toddler's snot going the wrong way. I felt lumps on my face and as I moved my fingertips brushed by bits of floating dirt. My feet, kicking out helplessly, found no bottom to stand on, just more depth, more filth, more disgusting, disgusting filth. It was dark in the cesspit. Too dark to see. I could only smell and feel. As I brushed my arms back and forth in the waste I felt nothing but soft, mushy lumps. I grabbed them but they folded and oozed in my hands. I needed to find the knife!

Then I realised it had probably sunk to the bottom.

I took a deep breath and let my head submerge under the filth. I felt the lumps and the gritty shit run up my face and into my hair. My nostrils filled with it. I felt it in my ears. And the perimeters of my eyelids burnt as the waste tried to enter.

I held still for a moment and felt my body drift slowly downwards.

Deeper and deeper...

How much further could I go?

I sunk and sunk and sunk while bits ran up my sleeves and trousers.

Eventually my feet touched the bottom.

I was choking now.

No breath left.

FOR THE LOVE OF GOD, DON'T OPEN YOUR MOUTH!

I felt around on the base of the cesspit, running my hands back and forth, touching the rusted metal.

YOU'RE GOING TO DROWN! I thought, feeling my head swelling under the pressure.

And then I felt it. A solid lump of steel. In the darkness I held it in both hands and opened it. It was the knife!

I kicked off from the bottom and felt myself rising through the waste.

In the back of my mind I imagined some hellish hand grabbing me and pulling me back down, but instead I rose up.

As good as that was, I couldn't hold my breath any longer.

Oh Jesus...

My mouth opened and I felt the crappy-gloop pour in like a burst dam. It ran between my teeth and settled on my tongue. Lumps – gritty and sandy. When I shut my mouth it was like mush. Like a demonic slush puppy.

Finally my head emerged. I spat the contents from my mouth and threw up.

Then I raised both hands, brown and dripping with shit, up towards the lid of the cesspit. I gripped the rusted iron lid and pulled, ignoring it digging in.

I hauled myself upwards and the night air had never smelt sweeter or cleaner. I fell onto my face but I could still smell the pit. I gagged, hocked and hocked and threw up some of the waste I had accidentally swallowed.

I grabbed the substation and hauled myself up. I paused for a moment and tried not to think about what I had just done. I wanted my brain to make no memory of it. I wanted it to be a bad dream that *I was sure* did-not-happen. I would burn the clothes. Bathe for a week. Write and read and drink and forget.

I closed the iron lid and stamped it shut. Then I walked back.

Outside of my flat I saw the Romanian family talking to the landlady.

Neither of them said anything to me.

They just watched in silence as the shit-covered-man walked past holding a knife.

In fact they only seemed to be *half shocked*, as if this kind of thing was expected of me.

Back in the flat I tried to have a shower, but the water wouldn't run.

Then I tried the bath, but it also wouldn't run.

I sighed.

By the door, amongst the post, was a letter from the water company:

Dear Sir,

Due to persistent refusal to pay your water bill we have terminated your supply.

I sighed again and grabbed my phone. I called Joe.

"Joe, I need a favour."

"All right, mate. What is it?"

"I need to shower at your flat."

"Okay. And by the way, I'm sorry about earlier. I –,"

"Forget about it."

"I just told Shannon the truth. I felt so bad about it, considering how much you helped me. She's forgiven me. She called the police and explained it's all a big misunderstanding.

That's some good news, I suppose, right? You won't have to get the knife back. Good news, right?"

"Joe... forget about the shower."

"Are you sure."

"Yes mate. It's probably best if I don't see you for a while."

Larry Sparkle

Larry walked into Galway Castle at midnight. The bouncer didn't ask him for ID. He didn't search him. He didn't question his trainers when it was strictly a *shoes pub*. They knew each other. The bouncer was a bad man. He enjoyed battering drunken young men. He got off on it, during the beatings and then later, alone, when he reflected on it. He was a bad man. And all bad men in Birmingham knew Larry.

Larry had just broken halfway through his second gram of cocaine. It was nicely tucked between a twenty in the breast pocket of his Fred Perry jacket. He patted it, just to be sure. He did this every few minutes. The paranoia had set in long ago and was now in full swing. He was looking for someone in particular, but Galway Castle was packed. The air stunk of cheap aftershave and belches of lager. His face was a bowie knife and his eyes, box jellyfish blue, cut through the crowds trying to find who he was after. Whoever they were, they were the unluckiest person in Birmingham.

Because The Night was playing and Larry liked Patti Smith. He paused momentarily and danced to it. An old slag he half-remembered rubbed up against him on the dance floor. She alluded to a messy fumbling the pair of them had had the year before. Larry nodded, left, ordered a vodka tonic and began prowling. His blood was up.

"Quick word, mate," he hissed in the ear of a young man in the smoking area.

Dennis turned quickly and saw Larry. He had been found. "Oh, you all right Larry?"

Larry nodded and slowly slid his arm up the inside of Dennis'. He gripped firmly and smiled, repeating the same demand. *Quick word.*

The two men left the smoking area. Dennis hadn't finished smoking, so he had to throw his roll-up on the floor. A woman noticed this and paid attention. She noticed the worry on the younger man's face. She noticed the way the older man with the blank face seemed to *lead* him away. He didn't look like a copper. He didn't look like a bouncer. It was strange. Not completely out of the ordinary. But it was strange enough to notice.

"What's this about then?" Dennis asked but he already knew. He was just hoping.

Larry led him through the crowded pub and towards the door. The bouncer held it open for him and Larry nodded as he passed through. The five-series was parked on the double yellows just opposite the pub. Dennis was saying something, being coy and playing dumb, but Larry wasn't listening.

"In you get," he said to Dennis and opened the back door.

"Wait, please, Larry. Can we just quickly talk before –,"

He put his hand on the top of Dennis' head and forced him in. He shut the door. The central locking trapped him. Larry lit a cigarette and leant up against the back window. The bouncer was nodding at him, but he ignored. He smoked the cigarette, watching the sky. Then he quickly keyed up some more coke, got into the car and drove away.

"You're going to withdraw five hundred quid."

"Okay, fine mate. That's absolutely fine," Dennis had his head in his hands. Then he straightened up quickly. He was twitchy and sweating. He was terrified.

Larry parked at a petrol station at the top of the road. "Five hundred," he repeated.

"That's fine Larry, honestly."

"Don't mess me about."

"I won't."

"Or I'll drive to your mother's house and rape her," he paused for a minute and then said the name of the road she lived on: "Webb Lane."

In the back seat, Dennis froze. He looked at the eyes in the rear-view mirror that looked back at him. They didn't blink. They meant everything that had just been said. So he got out of the car quickly and ran up to the cash machine on the Texaco wall. Larry was watching. The radio was on low, so Larry turned it up a little bit. He didn't recognise the song, so he took the opportunity to check on his drugs...

They were all gone.

He threw the white speckled twenty into the footwell and grinded his teeth. His blood was up higher now. He grabbed the steering wheel and squeezed it until his hands cramped. So instead he curled his toes until they burnt. Something inside him needed to be released.

"Five hundred," Dennis said when he returned and held a handful of cash through the driver's window.

Larry was out of his mind. "Another."

"What?"

"Another five hundred."

Dennis looked confused, or at least tried to. He knew what Larry wanted. He knew that his card limit wouldn't allow it. What he didn't know was that Larry knew that as well. He didn't want it to. He wanted an excuse.

"But, I can't. I –,"

Larry got out of the car and forced Dennis back in again. This time Dennis protested. He screamed and kicked so Larry broke his nose and shoved him into the back. Dennis was stuffed between the front and back seats, crying and moaning, pleading and bleeding. The man that owned the petrol station watched from behind the counter. He saw plenty working where he did. So he soon forgot.

The Bullock pub was on the Stratford Road. It took the five-series only a few minutes to get there. Larry parked the car in the most shadowed spot. He reminded Dennis what would happen if he played up. Then he stepped out, the five hundred inside his Fred Perry and the crumpled twenty in his back pocket. Maybe he would bump into another dealer. He locked the car.

"Where's Tommy?" Larry asked a kid in the smoking area whose face he recognised.

"Inside."

Larry pushed the door open and walked in. He spotted Tommy and walked over to him. Tommy saw him coming and took a gulp of Carling before standing. They shook hands.

"How'd you get on?" Tommy asked.

"Got it," Larry stuffed the wad into Tommy's side pocket without anybody seeing.

"Did you hurt him?"

"Not really."

"Where is he?"

"In the back."

"What d'you mean?"

"In the back of the car."

"Fuck sake, Larry. Don't bring him here."

"What do you want me to do with him?"

"I've got the cash now. I couldn't give a fuck."

"You don't care?"

"No. Get rid of him."

Larry turned on his heels and walked outside. He lit another cigarette and watched the car. Then he threw it away and started walking across the car park.

He hadn't decided yet.

The Happy Boerboel

Alright, cunt?

My name's Melvin.

I enjoy shitting in nettle bushes and chewing on the airwaves of squirrels.

I live in Sarehole park and I am a Boerboel, also known as a South African Mastiff.

Pleased to meet you!

This morning felt strange as I yawned myself awake, napping near some bones. The day felt as though it was bringing something with it – something bad. Today is not going to be your day Melvin!

"How come?" I asked the tattered bones in front of me, wondering if they would reply or not. But they chose not to. "Suit yourself."

The grass in the park was covered in dew and I breathed in fresh air through my black nostrils. I scanned about for things to do but it was early and probably a weekend, so the humans didn't come until later.

I padded across to the car park and saw a van parked up. Two roofers were sat inside. They were eating bacon sandwiches. One with…

Sniff

Sniff

Brown sauce and black pepper.

The other with...

Sniff

Sniff

Fried tomatoes.

I licked my slobbering lips and crawled underneath the open van window. They couldn't see me. I lay still for a minute, sniffing softly and listening to their radio. The DJ was appealing for information on a missing postman.

"That's fucking weird, ay it?" One of the roofers said.

"I know, aye," replied the other.

"They reckon the poor prick was last seen walking through here."

"Really?"

"Yeah. Then he just fucking vanished."

(I'll spare you the tension. Yes. I killed him. And then I ate him. I even ate his letters he was delivering. But I nearly choked to death on a fiver someone had been sent for their bar-mitzvah. Come to think of it, I've never ate a Jew. That could be interesting... What do you call those dreadlock things they have? Maybe I could use them as dental floss for afterwards?)

The smell of bacon was becoming too much to handle. I felt long strands of drool dangling from my jowls and collecting by my feet.

Enough fantasising about eating an Israeli...

GET THE FOOD!

"GIMMIE! GIMMIE! GIMMIE!" I roared, jumping up and reaching through the window at the roofers. They both screamed and fumbled to get the van started. I was foaming at the mouth when I stuffed the nearest sandwich into it.

OH SHIT! TOMATOES! I HATE TOMATOES!

I regurgitated all over the roofer who was pissing his pants at the sight of me. But before I could grab the other sandwich, the van pulled away.

Dust kicked up as it tore out of the car park and back onto the road. I sat and watched it, extending my leg to do a quick piss. Cowards! I thought to myself briefly, before heading back into the park.

For a few hours I napped under a pair of oak trees in the middle of the park. The humans used them as goal posts and sometimes I would watch them running about – succulent thighs, firmed young calves – it was making me hungry.

One night a gang of stoners sat between the trees and shared a few funny fags. I had crept up on them. It was dark and they were delirious, so it wasn't very difficult. They thought I was a hallucination to begin with, until I stole a kebab. If the sauce hadn't been laced with THC then I would have killed them all. They were lucky. Instead I just lay half-conscious on a lap and they took turns petting me. I never did see them again.

I've lived in Sarehole park as long as I can remember. My first memory is faded but I can still remember bits-and-bobs. It was a rainy day when my daddy took me down to the river. He was wearing his favourite shellsuit. "You're no good!" He said to me, as I pined and pined for him. "Nutty dogs, you are! The whole litter!" Then one by one he threw my brothers and sisters into the fast-flowing water. Not me! I thought. And I sunk my baby teeth into his wrist. He dropped me and I padded away as fast as I could.

Since then life has been the same... a never-ending cycle of child eating, mauling, sleeping and stalking. Squirrels are nice. I like watching them from the shadows. They look so innocent and cute.

I must have looked *innocent and cute* at one time too, before cruelty turned me murderous.

I love the sound squirrels make when I sink my jaws around their necks and start shaking. The noise only lasts a moment. They're so weak and easy to kill. The noise is a cry for mercy, but it excites me so much I can't help clamping even harder and snapping them in half. Sometimes I don't even eat them. I just kill them for the fun of it. But boy, I tell you, I wish I could hear that noise for just a little while longer.

Anyway, like I said, squirrels are nice (...*to kill,* I mean). But children are my favourite.

They make a similar noise.

I fucked up on the first child I tried to devour. Her mother was a few feet away and I didn't see her. I was young and cocksure when I grabbed the little bitch around the ankle and pulled her to the ground. I sheared all the flesh off her leg, but before I had a chance to pounce, I felt a stab in the ribs. The mother had kicked me with her high-heel. Shit, it hurt! So I retreated to the safety of the trees.

I watched the mother carry her injured pup away and I cried. Not from the pain of the wound in my side. No, not that...

Where had my mother been for me? Why didn't she protect me? Why didn't she love me?

The useless bitch!

(literally)

The police came to the park that night. They prodded the bushes and let Alsatians sniff about for me. But I have no scent. I am not of this world. That I am sure of. Nothing is as wicked as me.

The next morning I looked at posters they put up. I sat in front of them for hours, smiling and wagging my stump (where a tail used to be).

The drawing was quite good, but they made me too small. I had bigger shoulders and darker eyes, my ears were pointier like devil horns and my jaw line was stronger.

It read:

DANGEROUS DOG

On 13/10/17 a young girl was viciously mauled by an unidentified dog.

Witnesses remarked on the size and ferocity of the animal.

Please be vigilant.

DO NOT WALK THROUGH THE PARK ALONE!

DO NOT WALK THROUGH THE PARK OVERNIGHT!

DO NOT APPROACH THE ANIMAL IF YOU SEE IT!

I felt notorious.

But the next time I did it – they didn't find the child. And no one made the connection with the dog attack some months before.

I pulled him into the bushes by the river and ate him alive. I crushed his windpipe to stop him from screaming. It took me two days to eat him all, in the privacy of the bushes, away from the police and search parties. I gnawed on his bones, sucked at the marrow and grinded and chewed it all away to dust and sludge. Then I shit him out by the road. After a few days it dried-up and blew away. I saw some people stand in it. They cursed themselves, like: *Bollocks! I stood in dog shit!* Not knowing it was the remains of a dead child.

Once a mongrel caught sight of me and left his owner behind. He followed me, hopping through the bushes and disturbing me as I tried to sleep. I supposed he'd never seen a Boerboel before. He asked if I wanted to play, so I sunk my teeth into his eyeballs. One. Then two. On the second I manage to rip the retina out, but I didn't like the taste of it – it was like rubber. Stupid mongrel. The *Missing* signs labelled him as a *Cockapoo*. A FUCKING COCKAPOO? Oh please...

The screams always make me feel better.

They make me feel better about the screams that *I* used to make.

Like when daddy tried to drown me.

Like when those kids doused me in petrol and set me on fire.

Like when those drug addicts cut my tail off with a Stanley knife.

Like when those gypsies set their Bull Terriers on me for fun.

I used to scream. I used to be the victim. Now I am the victimiser.

I am Melvin and I make the bastards scream!

"Oh the memories!" I sighed, somehow content with how life had turned out.

How could I lust for something better? I've never known any different. All I've ever known is pain and suffering and now all three of us are quite well acquainted, good friends even.

Resting my head on the grass I decided to nap. Maybe today would be a good day after all, even with that odd feeling in the morning air...

"THERE IT IS!"

My ears picked up as I heard shouting.

Something was going on.

I saw men running across the park towards me. It was the roofers from earlier, only they had brought friends with them. There were six. They had hammers, wrenches and pieces of pipe. They had come back to kill me.

"LET'S KILL THE FUCKING THING!"

"SMASH ITS UGLY HEAD IN!"

Before I had a chance to move, they surrounded me.

What had I gotten myself into? Was this the end?

I growled at them, a noise summoned up from the deepest pits of hell. They began second guessing themselves, more so when they looked into my dark eyes, devoid of any soul or mercy.

I leapt forwards and they split, giving me an escape route. I was no fool. I stood no chance against all six of them. So I darted quickly through the gap and began charging across the grass.

"GET IT!"

"DON'T LET IT ESCAPE!"

I heard boots crunching into dirt behind me. I could smell unforgiving steel, and *smell* was enough! I didn't want to *taste* or *feel*.

At the edge of the park I descended into my hiding place by the river, but stocky figures clattered through behind me, stamping bushes flat and snapping branches out of their way. I was in trouble. I needed to think. Surprise them! The nearest man to me wasn't expecting me to turn. So I did.

Turning quickly, I planted my head into his crotch. It smelt unwashed and stagnant. So I sunk my jaws around his bollocks and shook. An operatic scream went up as I pulled his testicles out of their sack and grinded them to mince.

"IT'S BIT OFF TREVOR'S PENIS!" One of them shouted.

I let the bastard loose and carried on, deep into the undergrowth and edging towards the end of the park. Here I built a lead on them, but my hands and feet were ripped raw by thistles and hawthorn. I was sweating and exhausted when I crawled out the park. I wanted to rest but I could hear them getting closer – still raging with bloodthirst.

In front of me was the bridge. It stood over the river.

The costume was beginning to itch me now and my back muscles had locked-up.

I stood up and ran over to the bridge, bending down and creeping under.

Boy was I stiff! My back could only manage so many hours on all-fours.

In the shadows I watched the men smash hawthorn to pulp, before emerging and looking about.

I started pulling the Boerboel costume off, fumbling in the darkness to find the black sports bag I hid under there. It was full of my normal clothes. When I found it, I put on the tracksuit along with the trainers and baseball cap. I had shape-shifted.

When I looked back the men were still there, scanning about and swearing. Regardless, I took my chances and crawled out anyway...

"OI!" One of them shouted at me, wrench-in-hand. "YOU SEEN A DOG ROUND HERE?"

"Erm, no I haven't..." I muttered.

"AH LEAVE HIM!" Another one said. "HE'S JUST A FUCKIN' RETARD!"

Phew!

I smiled. My brow was ice cold with sweat and my hands were still trembling.

That was a close call! Take a few weeks off! I tried to tell myself.

But I knew better.

I knew the temptation would become too much, as it always did.

Before soon I would return to the park.

Dressed as the Boerboel.

And ready to eat some children.

Claw Hammer Romance

A week later I had been assigned some work labouring on a building site. It was hard work. But it offered to burn off my settee-stomach and get me away from the bottle. Nevertheless, I found myself drunk on a weekday and watching Hubert cooking. He kept putting broccoli on the pizza and I was screaming at him to stop.

I was comatose on the couch, leafing through the post and dying of an alcoholic hunger – two, maybe three days without any food at all – awoken by a crippling sobriety. My stomach had been knotted and my intestines were crying out to me.

"These Doctor Oetker's are the best!" Hubert was saying as he smiled down upon the thin-crusted pizza like some weird, gimp moon.

"Enough broccoli!" I shouted through the suds of a can.

Hubert Moccasin had been living with me for two days. He was an enormous black man, as wide as he was tall, a shining orb of a head and hands like breezeblocks. He was on the same building site as me and needed some digs, so I agreed to have him. I didn't ask why. I liked him. He was insane. And that was why I liked him.

In fact, when we first met, he introduced himself as: *"Hubert Moccasin, like the hat."*

He was also obsessed with food to the point of lunacy.

"That shop is great! Just great!" He kept going on about the outdoor on the corner. It was my local for booze, but when I showed Hubert he started buying crazy shit like papayas, turkey-ham and pumpkins. "Twenty per cent off turnips!" He boomed as he carried on with the broccoli.

"Don't buy anymore fucking turnips!" I said, glaring at a large pile of them in the corner.

As I stared at the turnips, an idea suddenly hit me:

I bet he shoves them up his arse.

I bet he shoves them up his arse and waits for me to eat them.

I eyed Hubert suspiciously. "I'm not eating those things! You're wasting your time!" I said, but he didn't pay me any attention.

Finally, after adding needless toppings, the pizza was ready to be put in the oven. But there was a problem. "It don't work! It don't work!" Hubert started saying as his fat fingers twiddled at the dials.

My mind cleared for a moment and I remembered the oven had never worked in the flat, only the hobs. I had always microwaved or toasted things.

I told Hubert this, and he started frying the pizza in a pan. At this point my appetite left me. I had work in the morning – early. And there was a heat wave roaring through Birmingham. I needed sleep.

"You're not having any?" Hubert asked when he saw I was heading to bed.

I glanced over my shoulder and saw smoke billowing up from the pan. "No Hubert. You have it all."

"Suit yourself."

I went to sleep.

And dreamt about turnips.

The next morning I found Hubert unconscious on the couch. The smell of fried pizza still lingered in the air. That, along with the cheap alcohol rotting inside me, turned my stomach. The sky and day alike, seemed stale. I knew that shovel and mortar awaited me, along with eight hours, sweat, boredom… another day of my life gone without purpose.

"You're over thinking again," I said to myself as I began to walk.

Pigeons were waiting outside the flats. They flew away when I slammed the security door shut. I watched them escape and I envied them. *Envying a pigeon!* How shit must your life be to envy pigeons? I lit a cigarette and tried to shield it from the rain. Then I thought about the book I had been reading in bed before passing out (whilst Hubert mutilated the Italian cuisine). *Less Than Zero* by *Bret Easton Ellis.* I was a fan of his. I liked the rawness of his writing and I liked to glimpse into the life of spoilt American rich kids.

I wanted to drive a Porsche.

I wanted to sniff cocaine.

Yet *I* was wandering through the rain, smoking a stolen cigarette and on the way to a muddy building site.

During this walk I performed my morning ritual – rethinking existence.

Where to be? What to do? With who? But lack of effort soon diminished any possibility.

"...Fuck it."

I carried on.

On the building site two old houses had been knocked down. Footings had been dug for two new ones and we were in the middle of laying blocks in the ground. I was labouring for the brickies and I hated it. I hated bricks. I hated bricklayers. I hated mortar. I hated shovels. I hated... I just *hated.* Better than anyone alive or dead ever had. That was my talent. Hatred.

Before the houses had been torn down, I checked inside for anything of value. All I retrieved was a Farthing coin from under a floorboard. It was dated 1888.

I traded the coin with Shouting Dean (a partially-deafened football hooligan) for a packet of crisps. He had started walking around the site, telling everyone how he'd sell this ancient penny and become rich. It was however worthless. Only I didn't tell him that. Instead I ate the crisps.

But that morning Shouting Dean was nowhere to be seen. I paused by the main gates and looked at the handful of stragglers that were milling about. They were mainly labourers – the deadbeats, the tramps, pissheads and pillheads trying to shake hangovers or comedowns before work started. That, or they were the arselickers. They wanted the foreman to see them bright and early, strutting about with a shovel in hand but not actually doing anything at all.

The view bored me – irritated me, even. I felt a twinge in my heel to try and turn me away from the abyss I was being drawn into, but I fought it. I fought the apathy and burning intolerance I felt for my fellow man. I needed money.

So I shut my eyes, inhaled the filth, and began towards one of the cabins used for dinner.

Inside I stole some coffee. I didn't like coffee. But I stole it anyway.

Maybe it'll wake me up! I thought, feeling groggy or maybe a tad drunk. While I made the coffee, I thought about Hubert. How would Hubert have his coffee? Probably with turnip pulp.

I sat down and sipped at my beverage just as the foreman walked in. He was a repulsive little shit of a man with no jaw-line or arse to speak of. I wasn't interested in his arse, I just noticed he didn't have one. Instead it was just a sagging, endless back that at some point turned into thigh. The man was clearly a cunt. And his ounce of power, telling nobodies like me what to do, made him a legend in his own mind. He glared at me, so I looked back and sipped at the drink. In his podgy face I saw every teacher, every bully, every copper. Then he started:

"Why are you in here, drinking tea while the other men are working?"

"They're not working. And this is coffee."

"They *are* working. And I don't care what it is."

"Okay."

He looked at me in silence.

Maybe he thought his glare would force me outside.

When in reality, the only thing it would *force*, would be my fist through his front teeth.

"Get outside," he demanded.

"I'll be out in a minute."

"The men need muck!"

I threw the coffee mug into the sink and walked past the no-arsed-Nazi. Every foreman I ever worked for had been the same. I never managed to tolerate any of them. It was a stubbornness I had. A proudness. A curse.

Outside I was met with damp, clay air. Hubert had also arrived. He was eating something and talking to the bricklayers. Hubert, like me, was a labourer, but only on his payslip. He worked about as hard as he cooked well. But no bricklayer (or short-arsed-Nazi) dared say anything to him. He was big and unhinged. And that was why I loved him.

"MUCK!" I heard someone call. It was Shouting Dean.

He grinned at me and stuck a mangled thumb up into the air. (It had been partially bitten off by an Aston Villa fan the year before.)

I smiled back and grabbed a shovel. I would labour for Shouting Dean. He, for some reason, I could tolerate.

I noticed the rain was beginning to die off and it made me feel sad. Rain could always end the day early but now it wouldn't. This meant a muddy site, damp clothes, slipping and sliding and late finishes. The ground was red clay. So, although it was solid during warmer days – it took only a few hours of drizzle for it to become like a bog. It held water, making it heavier to shovel and it became like glue, impossible to get off the shovel once you had it on. What it loved to do most however was gather up on your wellingtons.

I tried to distract myself and threw a mix on. Then I lit a cigarette and spoke to Shouting Dean with fingers in my ears. I asked him what he'd done the night before:

"I ONLY WENT AND SMASHED THE FUCKING PUB UP!" he said.

I nodded and smiled. I wasn't really interested, so I looked away...

And when I did, I saw something much better:

A woman was walking across the site. Was I daydreaming? A woman? With legs. And a pulse. Breasts and all the rest. She looked good at a distance and okay up close. For some reason she was coming at me. To begin with I thought it was the alcohol abuse finally catching up – delirium.

"Hello," she said.

I nodded.

"Is Greg here?" she asked and while she did, I took a quick, hard stare into her face. She looked in her early forties but still attractive. The evidence of *something* was there – a divorce maybe? Wrinkles had transcended from marked into etched. She had just broken into the darker years of her life and her face was screaming it.

"Greg? I don't know who that is," I eventually said.

"The foreman."

"Oh, that prick. He's in the cabin, playing with himself probably."

She forced a look of mock disapproval before walking away. I watched as she did.

"Who the fuck was that?" I asked Shouting Dean.

"That's Trish. She does payroll."

"Oh yeah?"

"Yeah. Fit, ain't she?"

I shrugged. "Suppose."

I plunged the shovel into the bag of wet sand and imagined what Trish looked like with nothing on. The idea intrigued me. I started working harder.

At dinnertime I was smoking a cigarette and Hubert walked up to me. He was the cleanest looking labourer on site. Not a lump of wet clay on his boots or a speckle of mortar on his face. That was, of course, because he hadn't ventured out the cabin. Most often he went inside, helped himself to everyone's tea and then napped.

"Yo!" He said when he saw me.

"Yes, Hubert."

"What do you say to a Tudor meal?"

"What?"

"For tea tonight. I'll make us a Tudor meal!"

"That sounds lovely," I said and moved away from him quickly.

Had I been too hasty in letting Hubert stay at my flat? His obvious mental health problems were beginning to worry me. Then again, what could I do? Try to throw the big psychopath out? No way.

Inside the cabin I stood weary and filthy by the door and watched the other men tuck into their dinners. I hadn't brought anything myself. Not because I wasn't hungry, but because I had felt cautious about cooking in front of Hubert.

He did all the cooking. For all I knew he could have flown into a rage.

"OI, OI! DICKHEAD'S FORGOT HIS DINNER!" I heard someone shout at me.

I looked down the cabin and saw them. A gang of brickies who gave everyone on site a hard time. If the job wasn't hard enough already, they made sure it was.

"COME AND SIT DOWN!" Shouting Dean bellowed when he saw me. He was eating a tub of Scotch eggs. I went across to him and sat down. No one ever sat beside Shouting Dean – one, because of the shouting, and two, because they feared him. But I sat down and shared his Scotch eggs.

"You know something, Dean? I'm getting really fucking sick of those bastards."

"What bastards?"

"Them down there," I pointed down at the gang. They saw me pointing and started talking among themselves.

"So do something about it then," he said.

It's all well and good for you, you're a hard case! I thought to myself as I counted the scars across his face. Some of them were bright pink, others faded, others near invisible. Some were deep, others shallower. I had the feeling some of them were deeper in *other* ways. I'm sure they all told stories though, and none of them good.

"DICKHEAD LOOKS ANGRY!" Someone shouted.

A cackle of hyena laughter followed. It snapped me out of my daydream, and I realised I had been glaring at them the whole time. They were still jeering at me:

"Maybe someone else was flirting with Trish!"

(They must have seen me talking to her.)

"He's jealous!"

I was becoming frustrated. Close to something. You can only poke a dog so many times until it snaps, regardless of its temperament.

"Yeah he does look mad!"

"Reeeeeeeeeeeally mad!"

"I'm shitting myself!"

"YOU WILL BE..." I stood up and hurled the box of Scotch eggs at them. The snack-sized balls covered the gang like buckshot from some ridiculous shotgun. "...WHEN I LEAVE YOU TWITCHING AND BLEEDING IN A PILE OF YOUR OWN SHIT!"

The cabin silenced and everyone watched. Our animalistic ancestry exposed itself, through a perverse excitement to see what would happen next.

"Are you t-t-taking the piss?" One of them asked. He had gone red in the face, either from anger or embarrassment, and his voice had broken when he spoke.

"N-n-no I'm n-n-not," I mocked him, and people laughed.

He didn't like it. I had disrespected him in front of his friends.

"I'LL KICK YOUR HEAD IN YOU FUCKING PUSSY!"

"YOU'LL WHAT?"

"KICK YOUR HEAD IN! YOU GINGER CUNT!"

Wait. Now he was insulting *my hair?* I looked at his. It was thinning and dyed.

"I don't understand why a bald cunt, who dyes his shit wispy hair, would bring mine up?"

The whole cabin erupted in laughter. And he stood up. "SAY THAT TO MY FACE!"

Finally, the foreman tried to act like an authority. "Enough, girls. Dinner's over. Put that energy into your work!"

I locked eyes with my new nemesis and was certain that it wasn't over. Why did you do that? I wanted to ask myself. I took shit off them all day. I was a master at taking shit. Why? Because I didn't care. I didn't care about me, about them, about anything. I never felt insulted or angry – that required too much energy. Something had snapped in me, something that had been under strain for a long time. Ah well, I said to myself. At least work won't be as dull.

About an hour later a message got to me about the fight. I laughed when I first got the news. I laughed because it was like a playground affair, only with grown men. Either way, I told the messenger *okay* and got back to work.

Luckily, I was labouring for Shouting Dean and he gave me some pointers. I felt almost confident to begin with, practicing my left-hook by the mixer. My confidence drained however, when I saw my opponent stripped to the waist. He was carrying a hod-full of bricks up a scaffolding ladder. Jesus Christ! He was built like a fucking bull. In the cabin earlier he looked like a fat cunt with a hoodie on. But the sun came out, the hoodie came off and his physique was carved from English oak.

"Looks like you've got your work cut out," Shouting Dean said when he saw me staring.

I didn't reply. He was right.

It was fear sweat running down my face as I worked the shovel. I watched the droplets darken in the bag of sand and I was shaking. What the fucking hell was I going to do?

Later in the day, part of the footings caved in, so me and a few labourers had to jump in and clear it. As I was digging and worrying, I hit something hard. It made a metallic *ting*.

I pulled some clay away and saw the end of a claw hammer stuck in the dirt. No handle. Just the metal head. It was old and rusted but solid and strong. Immediately I knew what to do. I put it in my pocket and finished shovelling. Then I went to the thunder-box to test it.

In the darkness I grasped it between my thumb and index finger and pulled the glove back over. When my hand was balled into a fist the hammer was impossible to see. My hand looked normal... only there was a solid lump of steel within it.

This'll show him. I smiled sickly to myself, totally confident that my own physicality was far, far inferior to his. I needed to cheat. Fight smarter, not harder.

After work, those involved in the fight hung around. The foreman locked up and disappeared, so only a group of childish degenerates remained. Shouting Dean and Hubert Mockerson stood with me. My opponent and his gang were separate, along with a few other nosy fuckers.

"Where?" Shouting Dean bellowed at them, and they led us towards a field opposite the job.

There were horses in the field and they looked keen to witness the violence of us men. What animals! They must have thought. And they would be right.

"You ready then?" My opponent asked me. He was stripped to the waist again, but I didn't feel as intimidated as I had before.

I didn't respond. My mouth was dry. I just separated from the crowd and advanced towards him. He raised his fists – not like a prize-fighter but more like a seasoned pub brawler. I copied as best I could and tried to stay on the tips of my toes.

He came in quickly and I saw a hand come towards my face. I covered up and felt thuds on my arms. They were still strong enough to shake me about. He must have landed four or five before we went into a clinch. He was far stronger than me, so he quickly pulled me to the ground. We landed in a crash and the thump dazed me. I was suddenly dizzy and tasted grit in my mouth. He started punching or stamping on my head and at that moment I realised that *cheating* wasn't helping at all.

"Let him up! Let him up!" I recognised Hubert's voice.

The pounding stopped and someone pulled me up from the mud. I felt shaken and ready to collapse again.

"You're all right. Get back in there," someone said.

My vision cleared momentarily and I saw my opponent raise his hands again.

He was about six feet away and advancing towards me.

It was now or never...

I clamped down on the hammer and threw a right-hook as hard as I could.

My head was still spinning, but something connected. Something cracked.

Then something made a soft thud into the earth.

"FUCK!" Someone shouted.

I had thrown the punch with such force that my body followed. I collapsed onto the ground and lay for a moment before someone pulled me up. I was exhausted.

My opponent was lying a few feet away. He was flat on his back, his jaw twisted off at an angle and his eyes half-shut. His arms were stiffened, and his feet were twitching slightly. I had knocked him spark out.

Shouting Dean and Hubert rushed me to a local pub and before I knew it there were a dozen freshly poured, slowly settling Guinness's in front of me. I smiled a broken, bloody smile and let the black holy water rush down my throat and cleanse my soul.

"I never thought you had it in you," Shouting Dean said and shook his head.

"You didn't have any faith?" I asked.

"No."

Hubert kept slapping me on the back and laughing loudly. I wanted to tell him that he was hurting me, but I didn't... so he kept doing it. "You drink a lot," he said and pointed at the pints.

"Yeah."

"How much do you spend on it?"

"I only buy cheap stuff."

"Do you consider renting?"

"What do you mean?"

"Renting."

"Renting what?"

"The alcohol."

I didn't understand what he meant, so I ignored him. After a while of excited, childish discussions I excused myself to the bathroom. In a cubicle I removed the head of the claw hammer and dropped it out the window. It *clinked* in the alleyway, blending into the rest of the rubbish. Soon it would be cleared up and gone forever.

When I went back to the table, I saw a few of the nosy fuckers had arrived.

"He's in a bad way," one of them told me.

"Really?"

"His jaw is broken in *six* places. They reckon it'll never be right again."

I didn't care.

"Is he conscious?" Hubert asked.

"Just about. He won't be able to work for a few months. He'll lose his job."

I began to feel a twinge of guilt.

"He was crying when we left him. Worried about how he was going to pay the CSA for his two kids, the mortgage on his house, his mother's dementia care –,"

"ENOUGH!" I shouted.

My display of violence had built some respect, because they all shut up immediately. "If he had so much to lose then he shouldn't have been fucking fighting," I explained to the nods of both Shouting Dean and Hubert.

Turning away from the table I saw a familiar figure by the bar. It was Trish. She was wearing the same clothes from today and was staring right at me. I excused myself from the table and staggered over to her. I led a life of ceaseless staggering, either from brain damage or alcoholism.

"Hello," she said as I approached.

"Hello," I replied.

"I heard you got into some trouble after work?"

"How did you hear about that?"

"Greg told me."

"Who?"

"The foreman. You know, your boss? I think you referred to him earlier as *that prick*."

"How does Greg know?"

"Oh, I suppose some big-mouth was eager to spread the gossip."

"Shit. I suppose I've lost my job then."

"I talked him out of it."

"How did you manage that?"

"Greg has a slight... *fascination* with me. Don't worry. There's still a shovel there with your name on."

I felt like thanking her, but I didn't. The bravado from the bloodshed had other ideas:

"Do you want to come home with me?"

"Yes," she said quickly before draining her glass of white wine. I bought her another, a large, and told her I would say my goodbyes at the table. Trembling was already beginning in my trousers and I was giddy like a kid on Christmas.

When I reached the table I was smiling from ear-to-ear, but nobody else was.

"He's dead," Shouting Dean told me.

My smile dropped. And so did my erection. "*What?*"

"Brain haemorrhage," one of the nosy ones said. The other was crying. "I just got the call. He went to the toilet and collapsed. The nurses found him. They detected it too late."

I had killed someone! Just like Ted Bundy or Venus Williams. It didn't seem real. I thought maybe it was a sick joke, but the faces of the men weren't hiding anything, maybe only holding back tears. What a waste! A death. His life. Two fatherless children and now a deserted mother… and for what? To prove he was tougher than me? There was nothing to prove. He was!

I shook my head and started for the door. I couldn't be around any of them. I needed to be alone.

"OI!" Someone shouted.

I looked up from my feet and in the doorway was a large burly figure. I wiped my eyes and saw he was another brute of a man. He looked like my deceased opponent, and it clicked in my head just before the man confirmed it:

"YOU KILLED MY BROTHER!"

"Please, mate, I..." I tried not to start crying. Trish was watching.

"OUTSIDE!" He shouted.

"I didn't mean to! We were just –,"

"OUTSIDE!" He was howling. He was out of his mind. His eyes were ready to explode inside their sockets, and the veins pumping in his neck were straight out of a junkie's wet dream.

Someone put their hand on my shoulder and I turned quickly. It was Hubert. Shouting Dean was beside him. "You have to," Hubert said to me.

"What? I –,"

"It was his brother," Shouting Dean explained. "You owe him a fight. Win or lose."

I didn't have my claw-hammer – so I didn't have any bollocks. I gripped my hand where the hammer used to be but felt nothing more than soft flesh... a small, girlish hand trying to ball-up a fist. I was fucked.

Looking up I saw death, it was in the form of a rabid labourer with a mind full of murder. He wouldn't stop. He wouldn't lay off until I was dead.

"Okay," I said, turning and glancing at Trish by the bar. She was smiling seductively at me. The whole situation must have been thrilling for her. Maybe it wasn't the death of my previous opponent that was troubling me, but the embarrassment I would feel in front of her.

I walked ahead of the dead man's brother, into the brightness outside.

Then I ran away as fast as I could.

Running footsteps followed me. Several pint glasses broke around my feet. I heard shouting and swearing and car engines starting up. *Get in! Get in!* People were saying to each other. But somehow I made it home.

Hubert didn't come home that night. Trish tried to call me a few times. At first I thought it was the dead man's brother but she left a sympathetic voice mail. Maybe she was still interested? But I was too full of shame to call her back. I spent an hour on the internet looking how to block a number – then I did it to hers.

The next morning work called several times. Again, I didn't answer. The final voicemail from Greg told me I was sacked. He had bagged up some of my things and left them in the cabin to collect.

The police hadn't been in touch yet, but I was sure they would be.

The next evening Hubert Moccasin did come back – but only to pack his things. He ignored me to begin with and I ignored him.

When he was finished packing and standing at the door, he told me:

"Sorry, bro," he looked cold. "But I can't live with a coward." Then he went through the doorway and shut it behind him.

"Funny coincidence…" I said out loud.

First to the empty flat.

And then to the windy balcony.

"Neither can I."

Fresh Grotesque

One night I found a lump of my mom's hair stuck behind my foreskin. We used to share the bathwater. "YOU LOSER! YOU FUCKING LOSER!" I started shrieking at myself. I was *twenty-five* and pulling grey strands of my mom's hair out of my dick. "YOU PIECE OF SHIT!" I carried on as I towelled myself off, glaring at my pathetic existence in the bathroom mirror. "YOU'RE WORTHLESS! WORTHLESS! WORTHLESS!"

It was this *hair incident* that finally forced me to move out. I moved from embarrassment into abject poverty, but the latter still seemed more appealing.

One time I stole a sack of corn from the market and ate nothing but corn-on-the-cob for a month. A month of corn-on-the-cob! I had corn-on-the-cob with milk for breakfast. I had corn-on-the-cob with toast for lunch and I had corn-on-the-cob with corn-on-the-cob for dinner. It nearly drove me insane. But that fucking corn kept me alive.

In retrospect I think I was born to be a loser. The Johnny Thunders song *Born To Lose* had involuntarily became the anthem of my being. *Thank god for punk!* Punk justified my laziness and substance problems.

It was the same for some hippies I knew. They were lazy dope-smokers before they joined their *movement*. But the ethos suited them: no job, ganja all day, taking it easy. Joblessness and cannabis abuse just meant *not becoming part of the machine* and *coming closer to Mother Nature*. It was all complete bullshit. They, like I, claimed all the financial support and benefits from *the machine* that they needed. And as for the dope, well… usually cannabis was just the tip of the iceberg.

But regardless of whatever loser I was, somehow I had managed to land Steph.

Oh poor, poor Steph.

The fact that *I* had her, proved there was no God. How could there be? She was a stunner – 10/10 – smart, funny and infinitely kind (*…or gullible, should I say?*)

I got drunk every day in her Solihull mansion. I watched *Magnum P.I.* or *Dog The Bounty Hunter* on her TV, wanked to porn on her laptop, smoked weed she bought me, passed out in her bed, woke up and repeated. If God did exist, then surely he wouldn't allow such an injustice? Surely some charity worker who played with cerebral palsy children deserved blowjobs off Steph, not me?

But evidentially not. She fell for me – an arsehole punk alcoholic.

Most days I woke at noon. She'd been at work for hours by that point, at a recruitment agency. Ironic, isn't it? Her life revolved around finding people work, yet her own boyfriend was unemployed and happily so.

For the first six months I did whatever the fuck I wanted to. But then, as with most women in my life, she started to dislike my endless drinking. First, she tried to ban it completely. That didn't work. Then we went through thousands of insane compromises, before finally settling on one:

I had to walk to the off-license up the road for every single drink.

I couldn't buy a bottle.

I couldn't by a crate.

So from noon onwards, I was forever walking back-and-forth, up-and-down the road with a glass in my hand. The nearest off-license was *Papu's Wine Shop.* The owner was Papu Popu, a cheery old Indian man who happily agreed to what Steph and I suggested. Most days I bought a litre bottle of Cracken and a bag of ice. Papu would fill my glass and then I would walk home, half draining it on the way. I'd sit down, watch shit on telly, listen to my records, finish the glass and walk back again.

"Hello, my friend!" Papu Popu would say when I walked in. Then he'd snatch the bottle from under the counter, pour some into the glass and drop a couple of ice cubes in. This was my daily cycle.

Sometimes it infuriated me. Tom Selleck would be nearing a climactic end in *Magnum P.I.* but I needed to walk down to the fucking shop again. Steph took her car to work, so I couldn't steal that to drive down. Sometimes I tried running, but that always ended badly. Once I got ran over by a Ford Probe and another time I slid in dog shit and broke my glass.

But whenever I felt fed-up or annoyed all I had to do was remember my history and review my options:

Corn-on-toast?

Mom's hair down your foreskin?

"No thanks!" I'd say aloud. Then I'd gather myself up and carry on.

The situation at Steph's was like a real good drunkenness. A good drunkenness lasts about half-an-hour. You spend most your time trying to reach it, and then trying to get it back. That was the Steph situation – sweet but on borrowed time.

You see, Steph had two kids from her broken marriage. They were twin girls and spoiled to the core. They were little bitches who fucking hated me. And the feeling was most definitely mutual. Most mornings I would hear them outside the bedroom, pestering Steph about me:

"Mommy, he hasn't flushed again!"

"Mommy, he's left his dirty boots under the dado rail again!"

"Mommy, there's broken glass on the stairs!"

"Mommy, you deserve better!"

"Mommy, please bring daddy back!"

"Mommy…"

"Mommy…"

FUCK! I HATED THEM!

They were trying to ruin a good thing I had going. Don't get me wrong, I wasn't completely twisted and mental. I loved Steph. I wanted a good life with her. But I *didn't* want it to include those two precious bitches. So, one morning, unable to sleep and twisted on rum, I devised an evil plan…

"Morning, darling!" I beamed, walking barefooted and chested into the kitchen. I kissed her on the neck and heard the two bitches whispering from the breakfast table behind me.

"You're up early, babe. How are you doing?" She asked, finishing her breakfast and staring ever-loving at the scumbag before her.

"I'm fine, I'm fine," I said. "Can I talk to you quickly?"

"I'm in a rush, babe."

"I'll be quick. It's very important to me."

She looked intrigued and followed me into the hallway. I shut the kitchen door and took her gently by the shoulders. "I want to start helping more."

"What?"

"I feel like a cheap-skate, like a deadbeat. You're so kind to me and I don't do anything!"

"Well babe, Biscuit could do with some TLC…" Biscuit was the Labradoodle. "You know she is suffering terribly with her IBS at the moment…" Oh Jesus. "We have some *healing pampers.* When her rectum becomes inflamed –,"

ENOUGH.

"No! No! No! Not Biscuit. I want to help with the girls."

"Biscuit is entering the menopause, babe. She needs all our love."

"Yes of course she does. *But I want to help with the girls!*"

Steph held my stare. "Really? Why?"

"I want to get to know them."

"Oh that's so lovely!" She hugged me.

"I've decided that I'll drop them to school every morning, and pick them up."

"Oh but babe they get a bus. They like the bus."

"No, no, no. I won't hear anymore about it. I will take them to school."

She sighed. "But babe I need the car for work. And I've already paid a full year's bus pass."

I cut Steph off. She was beginning to irritate me. "Stephanie, it is done."

My plan was now in motion. She would do anything I told her to. My claws were deep into the crevices of her soul, and like a puppeteer I controlled her.

On the way outside for a cigarette I passed through the kitchen and glared at the two bitches eating their breakfast. (They had no idea what I had in store for them.) Outside on the patio I lit a cigarette and hummed a *Buzzcocks* song to myself. Biscuit, the labradoodle with the inflamed rectum, was playing with a chew toy by my feet. I kicked it hard in the ribs. It screamed and limped away quickly. I smiled.

The next morning I was in Steph's Mercedes, steaming drunk and singing along to *GG Allin*. I made sure to only play his *age appropriate material*. The bitches were sat in the back, dead silent and staring out the windows. I tried my best to infiltrate their thoughts, but my shamanism wasn't what it used to be.

"This isn't the way to our school," One of them said.

I ignored and carried on. She looked nervous, like she knew what I was planning. The other was just naively staring out the window, watching the roads and the streets go by.

"What are we doing here?" The first one asked when we arrived at our destination.

"Out."

"What? But this –,"

"I SAID OUT!"

The two of them scrambled out of the car. They hated me, but they were also terrified.

I had driven them to a vacant lot in Handsworth. Handsworth was the shit-clogged U-bend in the toilet plumbing of Birmingham city. It was full of heroin injectors, stranglers and general bastardry. The vacant lot was fenced off. At one time it had been a house or something, but it had been knocked down and left to erode. Weeds and mounds of old rubble were scattered around. This was perfect! I thought to myself. It was quiet and shady. I knew the area well from my crack-smoking, house-squatting days. That seemed like a lifetime ago. I wondered if Raoule Murphy, the Mexican-Irish drug pusher, still controlled the area? Probably not.

I rolled the Mercedes back in reverse and saw the two bitches standing nervously by the lot. They were looking at me with sympathetic eyes.

"What are you doing?" One asked.

"Wait here," I smiled, put it into first and began away.

I would never see them again.

...at least I hoped.

Papu Popu looked worried when I walked into his shop that morning. He thought I had died or something because I hadn't been sitting on the road waiting for him to open. I told him I had been busy and bought the bottle of Cracken and bag of ice as usual. He filled me up and then I walked back home. I thought about the two bitches and wondered if anyone had taken them yet.

I watched an entire season of *Diagnosis Murder* and drank the bottle of Cracken. My allowance from Steph was running low so I decided to get stoned rather than spend another twenty quid on rum. After a few joints I passed out and when I woke up later, I realised it would have been time to pick the girls up. I smiled. Then I wiped some ash off my lap and grabbed the car keys. "Surely by now!" I said out loud. Surely someone had taken them. Surely they were gone forever, out of this house, out of my life and out of Steph's. This meant she would be *mine* forever. I laughed to myself.

But when I arrived at the vacant lot in Handsworth, I saw what I dreaded:

The two bitches were still there.

"Please take us home!" One of them begged. The other one was crying.

"Get in," I muttered angrily into the steering wheel.

On the drive home I scared the shit out of them. I told them if they opened their mouths I would murder their mother and their shitting dog, and I would commit both barbaric acts whilst wearing rubber boots.

When we got home the girls ran up to their rooms. Steph tried to follow them, but I stopped her on the stairs.

"My god, what happened?" She asked.

"They had a rough day at school. We had a little heart-to-heart. They need some space."

Steph shook her head. "They love school. I don't understand."

"Steph..." I took her by the hand, walked her into the living room and sat her down. My Brandonian attributes were in full swing. "They told me some things..."

"What things?"

"They feel like they can't talk to you."

"Oh my god."

"They said you're always too busy with work. They feel like a nuisance."

"My poor babies!"

"It's okay, Steph. I spoke to them. We had a few tears between us. But I think I really got through to them. They want to spend some time alone. I think you should respect that."

"I've been a horrible mother!" She started to cry.

"Yes, you have. But I'll help you."

She cried in my arms and over her shoulder I looked at myself in the living room mirror. My face was rotten and twisted. Tomorrow! I assured myself. Tomorrow I'll be rid of the little whores!

"Now stop crying, Steph," I told her. "Go down the shop and get me a bottle of rum." She nodded and left. Then I turned the telly back on, lay back and smiled.

"GO ON QUINCY!" I cheered one of my favourite programmes.

I had to keep the volume high – to drown out the sounds of crying from above.

I came to my senses at the foot of the stairs. There was a glass of Cracken in my hand and I was fully dressed. What the fuck? I was unsure how I got there or what time it was. *What the fuck is going on?* I checked my phone and saw it was about half an hour until Steph and the girls usually woke up. I staggered to the downstairs toilet and splashed some cold water on my face. My hair was darkening at the roots. I needed to bleach it again soon.

"Come on my precious girlies! Time for school!" I shouted up the stairs but heard no reply.

I drank another glass of Cracken, then walked up.

"Darling?" Steph called me from the bedroom.

"Yeah what?" I slurred.

"The girls aren't feeling very well today. They don't want to go to school."

My back molars, rotten from sugary mixers, began to grind against one another. I burst into Steph's bedroom and squeezed my hand around her windpipe. "WHAT THE FUCK

ARE YOU PLAYING AT?" She pushed me away, falling back onto the bed and beginning to whimper.

"What are you doing?" she cried.

"I told you to leave them alone! You've damaged those poor darlings enough!"

"I just wanted to check on them! They said—,"

"ENOUGH!" I roared into her face, blinding her eyes with a spray of spittle. "I won't let you hurt them anymore! There's nothing wrong with them. They just don't want to speak to you. THEY-HATE-YOU! And THEY-WILL go to school today!"

I walked away from Steph and slammed the door on her crying. Then I stamped down the landing and into one of the girl's rooms. I saw the pair of them in the same bed, recoiling in horror and hugging beneath the covers.

"UP!" I commanded and pulled the sheets off them.

I made them get dressed, pack their bags and get ready. I was sobering up by that point, so I finished off the Cracken. The bottle was empty.

"Please don't leave us there again!" One of them cried as I fumbled with the car keys, trying to get the Mercedes running.

"Shut up!"

"Yesterday this man tried to take us away..."

"I said SHUT UP!" I got the Mercedes started and pulled off the drive. Something behind me blasted a horn but my eyes were too blurry from the drink. I just put it into first, turned *GG* back on and began towards the vacant lot.

I woke up in front of the telly. Biscuit was asleep by my feet, but I didn't have the energy to kick it or burn it with a joint like I usually did.

Whatever I'd been watching had ended. Some crappy cop show was on. A nerdy genius was bantering with a sassy black partner. I despised it immediately and turned it off.

Beside me was an empty space where a full glass of Cracken *should* have been.

I fumbled in my pockets and found my phone. It was three in the afternoon. I should have already set off to pick the girls up. My mind was blank. I had blacked out from the alcohol and couldn't remember anything.

"Shit," I cursed, growling and then spitting a big globular onto the tiled floor. I stumbled out into the hall, grabbed the Mercedes keys and put my Doc Martens back on.

I didn't listen to any music on the drive. I felt funny. My pulse was thundering in my neck. The windows were down, but a hot sweat had started on my forehead and spread to my feet. Fuck! They felt soaking inside my boots. I wasn't well. I was delirious. To begin with I could hear whispering in the back seats and fluttering around my head. Then at every junction I saw the front bumpers of cars jutting out before suddenly vanishing. "You need a drink," I said loudly to myself. Try some music to distract you! I thought. I put *GG* back on, but the lyrics were making me nervous and shaky. I had to turn it off. Focus on your breathing! A panic attack was nearing by the second.

When I arrived at the vacant lot, I was a mess. I felt like vomiting and passing out at the same time. But whenever I nodded, whispers and hallucinations frightened me awake.

There was no sign of the girls.

I soberly got out of the Mercedes and walked up and down the vacant lot, trying not to focus on what I had done. My mind, although panicked, was growing ever clearer.

It was not happiness I was feeling. Instead an equal measure of regret and dread.

"Fucking hell, man. Fucking hell," I kept saying to myself, attempting with a greasy, sweaty hand to light a cigarette. "Did you really do this?"

I walked across the road to a shop and tried to buy a miniature of rum, but I didn't have any money. I had spunked it all. The embarrassment sent me crazy and I ran out of the shop without speaking. Then I vomited beside the Mercedes, before noticing a car-full of shifty looking kids drive past me. They eyed me and the Mercedes up in a dangerous kind of way. You need to get out of here, I said to myself.

Driving back, I managed about five minutes before I had to pull off the main road and park up. I sat on the bonnet and focused on my breathing again.

WHAT HAVE YOU DONE? My sober mind asked, clawing through whatever remained of drunkenness and battling through the clouds of withdrawal. YOU JUST DUMPED TWO LITTLE GIRLS! I know… I know… YOU LET SOMEONE TAKE THEM! WHAT WERE YOU THINKING?

I got back into the Mercedes and drove back to the lot. Physically and mentally I began to feel slightly better. Maybe it was a higher power giving me some strength.

I rushed across the road to a row of dilapidated terraces that faced the vacant lot. "Excuse me! Excuse me!" I started banging on one of them.

An old lady answered the door and smiled at me. "Yes?"

"Did you see those girls across the road today?"

"Yes."

"Did you see where they went?"

"No."

"You have no idea?"

"No, I don't."

I nodded in appreciation and tried the next door. There was no one in. I tried the one after. The curtains stirred but no one answered. Finally, the fourth door opened. A young black woman with a baby in her arms answered and glared meanly at me.

"Watchu want?" She asked.

"Did you see those girls across –,"

"The road? Yeah I did. Don't know what two girls like that were doing round here."

"Did you see where they went?"

"Got in a van."

"What kind of van?" I stuttered.

"I've got to go," she started to close the door, so I jammed a Doc in.

"OI! GET YA FOOT OUT!" She shouted and the baby started to cry.

"Please, I'm sorry. What kind of van was it?"

"One of them old film rent vans!" she started slamming the door back-and-forth on my boot.

"What?" I asked desperately.

"Blockbuster! A Blockbuster van!"

I pulled my boot out and the door slammed shut. From the other side I heard locks click and chains be drawn across. It was probably wise to leave before someone called the police or a local street gang dealt with me.

In the Mercedes I locked the doors and tried to think... Blockbusters? A Blockbusters van? Blockbusters had been closed for years. No one even *bought* DVD's anymore, let alone *rented them*. I put my head into my hands and screamed. It was nearly five o' clock now. Steph would be home in half an hour and be wondering where the hell me and her two daughters were. I was in the shit. And the girls? I didn't even want to think what might be happening to them, soon or already.

I took my phone out and started searching for Blockbusters stores, if any, that were near to where I had left the girls. There was nothing. From what the last news article said, Blockbusters were to close all its UK stores. What the fuck now? Some creep could be driving around in a second-hand van.

Then at the end of the road I noticed a phone box.

I rushed down to it and if by some miracle found a yellow pages, half rotten and damp with urine. The front page had been torn off for roaches. I flipped through the pages until I found a list of Blockbusters stores. I tore out the page and stuffed it into my pocket. As I turned to leave, I saw a car had parked up by the Mercedes. That gang of kids were surrounding it and looking through the windows. I took the book with me and began to walk back.

"Is this your car?" One of them asked.

He looked about sixteen but was taller and stockier than me.

"Yes."

"Let us have a ride."

I belted him with the book. He fell off the kerb and his friends backed-up, so I took the opportunity to get into the Mercedes.

As I drove away, I could still see the kid, sitting in the road with blood pissing down his shirt from both nostrils.

This truly was the worst day of my life.

I longed for corn-on-the-cob.

The first Blockbusters on the list wasn't there anymore. It was a barber's, but I went inside anyway for clues. The woman who ran it was the humanised incarnation of cancer. She smelt like several thousand Rothman's blazing at once. Her eyes were jet-yellow and parts of her anatomy actually resembled the pictures on the back of fag packets, like lungs hanging out of people's throats.

"No bab," she croaked at me. "Nay been a Blockbustas ere for donkeys yehas."

I left before I caught leukaemia.

The second Blockbusters was derelict. The blue-and-yellow sign still hung above the pavement but the bulbs inside were long blown and the windows beneath were boarded with rotten plywood. I peered between the gaps but saw nothing inside. There was no sign of a van or anything else to indicate the girls were nearby. A homeless man outside the shop started vomiting and I heard spare change clanging on the ground. I could only assume he must have been eating copper coins. I left quickly.

On the drive to the third Blockbusters I felt my phone begin to ring. Breaking the law for the billionth time that day, I took the phone out of my pocket and saw Steph's face on the caller-ID. It was quarter past five. She was home late. Me and the girls were nowhere to be seen. Naturally she was panicking.

What to do? What to do?

Do I answer and give her some bullshit? Or just ignore it?

It was a lose-lose situation. So, I chose to lose in the way requiring the least effort: I didn't answer.

The next Blockbusters was the last one listed. But when I arrived I couldn't see it. I parked up anyway. The street was ghostly quiet, so I lit a cigarette and started mooching around. Traffic hummed in the distance and I felt anxious.

There was an alcove midway down the street with shutters half-down. It reminded me of an old shopping parade that had been sucked dry by some Americanised *mall* a few miles away. A golden calligraphy sign hung above the alcove. *Dahmer's Courtyard* it read. Below that was a big clock telling the wrong time.

When I passed underneath the shutters, I scanned around at the few shops that remained:

A closed music shop.

A fire-damaged Indian restaurant.

And further down... a Blockbusters.

"Oh thank you, thank you!" I said and walked quickly over to it. It was in the corner and almost hidden. The lights were on, the windows weren't boarded and the door was unlocked. Immediately I got the creeps.

From outside I couldn't see or hear anyone in the shop. But I recognised the posters in the windows:

Silence of the Lambs, Jurassic Park, The Matrix

They were all about twenty years out of date?

I pushed the door open and stepped inside. *Insomnia* by *Faithless* was being played on a radio show. DJs began discussing it when it ended, but *Insomnia* hadn't been in the charts since the nineties.

The whole situation tripped me out, so I carried on, walking between rows and rows of empty shelves, not a DVD or VHS in sight. It was like a labyrinth of grey plastic and blue carpet. The soundtrack to the nineties was keeping me company.

It all felt like a lucid dream until I finally spotted someone. There was an employee stood behind the checkout at the far end. He was stood dead-still and staring into space, not moving, not blinking, *not breathing* it seemed.

I paused for a moment and watched him. He was either ignoring me or in a trance. His hair was dyed brown and parted to one-side. His eyes were abnormally wide as if the lids had been stapled open. For a moment I thought he was a mannequin but ever so slowly I noticed the slight raising and deflating of his Blockbusters uniform. He was indeed alive.

"Excuse me?" I said and walked out from the shelves.

I crossed an open space to the counter, swerving between bins of movie snacks. I picked up a bag of popcorn as I passed and noticed the sell-by date was 2005. I threw it back.

When I got to the counter the man was still staring blankly ahead. I was stood in front of him, in his line of vision, yet his eyes seemed to stare right through me.

"*Excuse me?*" I repeated.

His face remained motionless, as if made of rubber, with a slight grin on his lips.

"EXCUSE ME!" I shouted again and saw a single bead of sweat run down his greasy forehead, settling into the curl of his smile.

"Yes?" He said softly.

"I'm looking for two girls, you haven't –,"

"The store is closed."

"I understand that, mate, but –,"

"The store is closed," he repeated.

I tried to continue but the man didn't say another word. He simply stood as he had before. Behind me I glanced to see what he might have been looking at. There was an old-style huge TV hanging from a wall bracket and playing *The Big Lebowski*. Apart from that, there was nothing.

When I turned back to face the man he was in the same position, only it seemed he had moved closer.

"Fine," I said quickly and went for the door.

When I got outside, I tried to remain calm. Then I walked back to the window and peered down the aisles at the main desk. The man was still there. Not moving. Not doing anything.

My phone buzzed and it made me jump. Steph was calling. This would be my second missed call. Should I answer?

I decided no.

Instead I left *Dahmer's Courtyard* and lit another cigarette.

While I paced back and forth, trying to decide how to break the news to her, I noticed a fenced off area beside the alcove. I walked across to it, partly out of curiosity and partly to distract me from the monumental fuck-up I had gotten into.

Peering between the mesh fences I noticed a parked van. On the side of it was a faded, blue Blockbusters logo. Could this be it? Were the girls here? I had no alternative. I had to check.

I threw my leather jacket over the razor wire and pulled my withered frame, decaying from booze and drugs, up and over the fence. For a moment my mind reverted to the days as a homeless crack-head, stealing and sleeping in the darkness of the city.

I landed hard on the ground and felt immediately unsafe. Eyes were peering at me from somewhere, eyes with malicious thoughts.

I peered in the van window but couldn't see anything, so I looked elsewhere. There was a padlocked door on the building that seemed to lead down to a cellar below the shop. I'd need to break in.

Across the road, opposite the alcove, some scaffolding had been erected around a building. So I left the yard and found a lose four-foot pole. With one heavy swing I busted the lock in half. It shattered and seemed to echo the entire foundations of the shop. I was sure he heard me. But I didn't have time to waste.

I opened the door and bolted into the darkness. My hand found a rail and my feet found steps, so I shot down them as quickly as I could. Something at the bottom was radiating light. I could see the glimmer of a bright room behind more doors. I threw them open and felt momentarily blinded.

As my eyes adjusted, I scanned around the scene before me:

It was like a nursery.

There were children's toys all over the place. The floor was like a felt play mat, with pretend train tracks and hop-scotch markings. The walls were painted with Disney characters in bright colours. And quietly, from some invisible speakers, nursery rhymes mumbled. I felt sick. A perverse suspicion was haunting my brain. "Please no," I whispered to myself.

The suspicion was confirmed when I saw a wall mounted video camera and a red-light flashing, recording....

"You sick cunt."

On one side of the room was a bed. It had *things* on it, but I looked away quickly.

"GIRLS!" I shouted. I didn't care about that weirdo anymore. I needed to find them. Please god, let them be all right. "GIRLS!"

I heard a muffled scream. I turned and saw something draped beneath a throw. I rushed over and tore it off. It was an animal cage. And inside, curled up and crying together, were the two girls.

"Oh thank god you're okay!" I panted hysterically, undoing the lock and pulling them out.

They recoiled from me and I didn't blame them.

"Did he do anything to you?" I asked.

"He put us in this box!" The one said.

"He said he would come back... please don't let him come back!" said the other.

"We're going home," I assured them. I grabbed a hand each and led them to the staircase. The darkness of the stairs was unnerving, but I didn't have time to worry. I swallowed a dry gulp and continued through the shadows towards the light of the moon in the yard.

As I stepped outside something caught me across the back of the head. My vision went from looking forwards, to looking at a concrete slab up close. I had been knocked down. The scream of the girls woke me from my daze and I rolled over. Just as I rolled, a four-foot scaffold pole bounced off the spot I was lying in.

The weirdo was standing above me, ready to swing it again. He wanted to cave my head in and take the girls back downstairs.

I rolled. Again and again. Each time the metal *cling* got nearer and nearer.

I rolled into the fence and didn't have anywhere else to go. As I pulled myself up, the pole caught me on the shoulder and something inside snapped.

I turned around and charged into him. I bum-rushed him with as much strength as my tiny frame could manage. I had a hand on each shoulder, pushing him backwards towards the door and the staircase. For those brief moments I looked into his face and saw that fucking smile was still on his lips.

The weirdo tripped over himself and went crashing down the stairs and into the darkness.

As our brawl ended, I realised the girls had been screeching for the entire time. Someone, the police or anybody, would be on their way by now. I had to move quickly.

With a broken collar bone, I lifted both girls over the fence and then myself. I rushed them to the Mercedes and started it up. As I drove away, I could hear raised voices shouting, probably bystanders investigating what was going on.

On the drive home no one said a word. The girls were cuddling in the back and my shoulder was hurting more and more as the adrenaline drained from my body. When we reached Steph's, I saw two police cars in the drive.

"Get out," I said to the girls.

I expected a *thank you* or *goodbye* but they didn't even look at me. They were out the door and up the drive as fast as their legs could work. From there I drove to Papu Popu's, parked up and went inside.

"Bottle of Cracken, Papu," I said and he smiled. "I haven't got any cash."

"Your credit is good, my friend."

I grabbed it off him and necked it hard.

"No! No!" he protested and tried to grab it back. I pushed him away and stepped towards the door. "Missus Stephanie will not be happy, sir. Please give it back to me."

"I'm off, Papu," I explained.

"What do you mean?"

"I'm going." He seemed confused. "I've got to see about murdering a man."

Baron of the Blue Bus

I'd been out of work for weeks and alcoholic solitude had begun to erode my brain. My writing had stopped dead and drinking had become, dare I say, *boring*. It was at this time that Wild Bill called me up. He was steaming drunk and told me he'd just *ate the best rump steak in town*. I corrected him. First for using a vile Americanism and secondly for putting *best* and *rump steak* in the same sentence. "Sorry, Wild Bill. There's just no such thing."

"Anyway, me mucker. Anyway, anyway…" He started rambling on the way he did. He would speak so fast he stumbled over his words – his mouth moved faster than his damaged brain could manage.

Wild Bill ran a local coach company. It transported children to and from school. It shipped retarded people around-and-about. And it even delivered dried, flaking pensioners to man-made beaches.

I was dubious about his call – and rightly so. He put it on me:

"I've got a job going on the coaches."

"Coaches?" I asked… delaying time, uninterested, worried.

"Yes, me mucker. The cowin' coaches."

"And?"

"And what?"

"What do you want?"

"To tell you about the job."

"What about the fucking job?"

"Well, me mucker. Well, well, well…"

"WHAT IS IT, WILD BILL?" I shouted down the phone. My patience had expired.

Then suddenly he started making sense: "It's a good gig. I'll start you on seventy a day," Every now and again his brain would correct itself and he would be able to communicate again. I often wondered what had rendered him so deranged. His jaw was off to one side and one eyeball bulged further out his skull than the other.

"Seventy what?" I asked him.

I needed to be sure. Knowing Wild Bill he could be meaning sultanas.

"*Powunds!*" He shrieked.

I thought for a moment.

Yes I was bored.

Yes I was skint.

I thought a little bit more.

Then I accepted.

Hung up.

Sipped my lager...

and regretted.

The next day, with a can of Tennents Super for company, I walked to the coach depot. It was early morning. Grey and drizzle. For once I appreciated that kind of weather – it seemed to wash away (or at least dilute) the hangover that was clinging to my bones like some third-world disease.

I passed by the canal and saw a homeless couple fighting. The man was old and decrepit. He was beating his woman by swinging a *Tesco's bag-for-life* into her. It was full of sleeping bags and pillows, so it did little damaged. I watched them for some time and smoked cigarettes. Then I came to my senses and carried on to the job.

The job!

Oh woe... the FUCKING JOB!

I knew it wouldn't last.

No way.

But maybe I could get a month's wage out of it? That would be something.

When I finally got to the coach depot, I found the front gates locked. After a few minutes of banging on them a man with a growth on his head opened. He seemed to know who I was without asking. This led me to believe the growth was somehow magical, like a crystal ball. Yes, that, or an extremely cancerous tumour that was killing him.

I strode out into the coach yard like a backward John Wayne. It was a dump. The tarmac had worn away under the weight of the coaches, leaving big craters of waist-deep rain water. It was like an assault course. And if the craters weren't enough, an enormous chained Rottweiler tried to maul me as I passed by.

"Looks like Henry doesn't care for you!" The growth man chuckled.

Across the yard were three separate buildings: a hut, a site office and a garage for the coaches. I walked into the site office and found Wild Bill.

He was doing tricep dips between two chairs and attempted to smile when he saw me. He said nothing, instead finishing his set before rushing across to his desk.

Wild Bill's long, grey hair seemed greasy and fake, like it was from a yak or some other creature. When he sat down he started shuffling papers and sighing loudly, opening and closing folders that had nothing inside them. I didn't understand what he was trying to do. Look busy? Or was he having another psychotic episode? Eventually he stopped. He attempted to smile again and asked me to sit. I didn't want to. But I did.

"Morning, me mucker!" He beamed.

"Morning, Wild Bill."

"So…" He began, stretching back and letting his fat ale gut slip from under his shirt.

"*So* what?"

"You think you've got the makings of a good coach driver?"

"What? No. Not at all."

"It's a hard graft. A *real* hard graft. It's not for everyone. No, no, no, no, no, no, no, no."

I didn't respond.

"But," he shrugged. "If you're certain… then I'll give you a shot."

"I'm not certain, Wild Bill."

After a few moments he stood up and shook my hand. "Welcome aboard! I'm taking a chance on you!"

I felt like begging him *please don't*. But I remembered:

Bills.

Rent.

Alcoholism.

(I didn't have a choice.)

"No need to start today though!" He shouted.

From a cabinet by his knees he snatched out a bottle of gin and two dusty mugs. I didn't like gin, but I drank it anyway.

While we drank, Wild Bill put on some *Creedence Clearwater Revival*. I sipped at my drink and watched him shout over the tannoy system at drivers in the yard. It was almost entirely nonsensical, slurred swearing and bad grammar:

"COACH FIVE! COACH FIVE! ...BRING ME YOUR ARSE!"

"PETE? PETE? DID YOU PUT THE SHIT HE DID INSIDE THE SHIT? HELLO? PETE?"

"SWAN-SEEEEEA, SWAN-SEEEEA, SWAN-SEEEEA!"

Jesus Christ! I thought. I needed to get the fuck out. But luckily for me Wild Bill was soon unconscious. He didn't respect the evil liquid. He was a glutton for it.

"That's the danger with the ol' spirits!" I said drunkenly and tried to stand up.

CRASH!

I tripped on some air and collapsed onto Wild Bill's desk. Everything on it went flying. Folders fell open on the floor and photos were knocked loose. They were all crappy 1970's porn and action shots of Ford Granadas.

Eventually I managed to stand and make my way to the door.

How does this always happen to me? I asked, ungratefully happy. I always managed to attract the psychos, the dregs, the shit and the annoyance. I was a magnet for it. A *bullshit magnet*.

Outside the site office I staggered across the tarmac, plunging and nearly drowning in multiple puddles and almost being mauled to death by Henry. It was like a scene from Platoon, or some other kind of adventure movie? *Indiana Jones and the Coach Depot Cretin.*

I made it out the gates. Then I stood and watched the coaches leave, for some reason I chose to wave at the drivers. I was holding back a torrent of vomit that was lying dormant (but bubbling) at the back of my throat.

"FUCK THIS GIN!" I finally proclaimed, bending at the waist and puking on a nettle bush.

On the walk back home, I passed by the canal and saw a floating *Tesco's bag-for-life* in the water. I regretted not just watching the homeless couple murder each other. Instead I HAD A JOB!

Back at the flat I put *The Kinks* on, lit a cigarette and tried to calm down. The iPod was on shuffle and the first track was *Dead End Street.*

"I can relate!" I slurred loudly.

Falling into bed I felt immediately groggy. I noticed my phone had a voicemail from Wild Bill. I played it and it made no sense. All I derived from it was to be back at the depot for seven the next morning.

Fine.

The next morning I was in a whirlwind of anxiety. It was *beer fear*, only from gin instead. (And that was worse!) I rushed around the flat trying to find my driving license, but I couldn't see it anywhere. I vaguely remembered swapping it with an Afghan man for some cannabis, but I couldn't be sure.

An hour later I found myself back at the depot. The same man with the growth let me in and I spotted Wild Bill feeding Henry some grey, oily looking meat. The look of it turned my stomach. I glanced around for nettle bushes to vomit in, but it was too late – Wild Bill had seen me.

"Morning, me mucker!" He shouted.

(I swallowed it back down...

in all of its chunky, salty goodness.)

"Erm... yes," I croaked.

He took me into a yellowy, headache of a room where a bunch of coach drivers were drinking tea and eating biscuits. He introduced me to them individually, but after every introduction would whisper a totally inappropriate comment into my ear:

"Here's Pat! ...*We call him Pat The Bag because he has no bowel.*"

"And this is Allan! ...*We call him Coco-pop because of the tumour on his head.*"

"This fella is Ian! ...*Shirt-lifter, poof, we reckon so anyway.*"

"And finally Barry! ...*Barry was a hitman for the Dudley mafia. Don't mess with him.*"

Barry was a fat old bastard with conjunctivitis in both eyes.

"Now...to your chariot!" Wild Bill took me by the arm, out into the drizzly yard and across to a row of big, blue coaches.

"Here's your baby!" Wild Bill said as he slapped the side of it.

He opened the door and we climbed aboard. I sat down on the driver's seat. The coach was chokingly hot and stunk of plums. I assumed one of the older drivers had last ridden it. The radio was playing some stupid Blitz-era song – a crackling woman's voice shrieking to the sound of strings.

"Have you driven a coach before?" He asked me.

"I can drive."

"Brilliant! You'll be driving the special children today."

"*Wait, what?*"

"They can be a rough crowd, me mucker. But don't worry..." Wild Bill pointed down to the peddles. "I keep a zinc pipe down there." And he winked. "Now, Pat The Bag will ride with you so you get used to the route, capeesh?"

"No. Wait. I change my mind. I don't want to anymore. I –,"

"Ah shutupa ya face!" He punched me on the shoulder. "You'll be fine." And then he left.

For a while I just sat there and felt sober – in thought and blood alcohol. What was I doing? Just WHAT THE FUCK was I doing? I put my head into my hands and tried to calm down.

"What's the worst that can happen?" I asked myself.

I don't know yet. But I will shortly... when it inevitably *fucking does!*

I punched the radio to turn it off but knocked the glove compartment open instead. When I went to close it, I noticed something inside. There was a half-full bottle of gin. Did God put it there? Or Satan? It didn't really matter. They were equally irrelevant.

A big, rubbery smile spread across my face as I snatched it up and took a long, hard hit.

I took another and watched Wild Bill re-emerge from the headache room with Pat The Bag. A third passed my lips before they could see me. Then I opened the doors and smiled drunkenly.

"Right, get going!" Wild Bill said.

I started up the coach and began on my journey. I found it surprisingly easy to drive. Maybe it was foolish confidence from the gin, but either way I got it out the depot and up the road.

The first thing I did was totally ignore everything Pat The Bag said:

"No, I said *right* here! You needed to go *right!*" He bitched.

"Okay."

I pulled into a cul-de-sac to turn around. As I did, an old couple in a huge beige estate tried to get past, blocking the rest of the road.

"Hurry up, you ignoramus!" The old man shouted, shaking his fist at me.

It took me fifteen minutes to get the coach out of the cul-de-sac. By then Pat The Bag was in a cold sweat. "Come on, come on! We'll be late!"

"I'm going! I'm going!"

Up the road we went, over a hill and past a golf course. A group of pensioners were preparing their caddies, so I blasted the horn at them.

"Don't do that!" Pat The Bag shouted at me. I ignored him and blasted it again. I was enjoying myself for some reason. But then we hit traffic. The road was ripped up and temporary lights were delaying everyone. "You see! If you hadn't got stuck back there we'd be on time!"

"Will you just calm down?"

"NO! The children will be upset!"

"And?"

"I'm not explaining it to them. You can! They're a handful when they're angry!"

"Jesus Christ, what are you *scared?*"

Pat The Bag didn't answer.

"You truly have *no guts*," I said to him.

A single tear rolled down his cheek.

"Oh for fuck sake…" I mumbled and focused on the road. What a moron.

After taking the wrong exit at a roundabout I finally picked up the first child. His mom was waiting at the stop and started some bullshit about me being late. Pat The Bag looked as though he was going to cry when he apologised but I, as usual, paid no attention.

"Is this a plane?" The boy shouted at me. "I want to fly on a plane!"

"You'll sit down and shut the hell up!"

He burst into tears and Pat The Bag had to comfort him.

Nevertheless, we were on our way.

Twenty minutes later the coach was full.

The kids were screaming because of my erratic driving and heavy braking.

"Oh man, oh man, oh man!" Pat The Bag stuttered beside me. "This is terrible, just terrible!"

"What is this fucking shit?" I asked as the Blitz-era song started to play again.

Managing to keep one eye on the road, I plugged my iPod into the stereo and put on *Velvet Underground*. However, my choice of *Venus In Furs* sent several of the children into panic attacks. Pat The Bag had to perform first aid. It was a nightmare and when he got back he was white and unsteady on his feet.

"Stop the coach!" He said.

"The fuck I will! I'm getting these kids to school! They need an education, don't they?"

"I'm going to faint! I need fresh air!"

I stopped by the side of the road and Pat The Bag got out.

He circled around some bollards by a shop, breathing heavily until he eventually collapsed on the floor and burst his shit bag.

I decided the kids shouldn't see such a thing. So I drove off and left him. In the rear view mirror I saw a flock of pigeons eating from his bag and dumping all over him.

Now I had no idea where the school was.

I shouted to some of the nearby kids, but they ignored me or started crying.

After a few minutes of driving aimlessly around and drinking gin from the bottle I parked the coach in the car park of a bowling alley. Then I got out and vomited all over a Honda Jazz.

"That man is crying porridge from his mouth!" One of the children observed of me.

Then, in a moment of pure apathetic insanity, I locked the coach door and did a runner.

Fuck it.

There was a pub just up the road.

The Old Man and the Lake

The bitch took everything.

I put my heart, soul and left pinkie (chainsaw accident) into my construction company but she even had that. I had to fold it. There're still two unfinished houses in Henley-in-Arden. Unfinished, because the bitch found herself a six-foot Turk with a magical shish kebab of a prick. *Omar* was his name and *oh man* did he fuck everything up.

"I'm leaving," she said one Saturday morning.

I was getting ready for the pub when she told me. I was doing up my donkey jacket and I took a long glare at the woman I once loved.

"Okay," was all I had the energy to say.

I hadn't loved her since forever.

There was a time (maybe even a *beautiful* time, to use a homo-curious word) that we were in love – truly. I still remember the feeling the first time I saw her. Man she looked good. Everything suddenly seemed totally irrelevant in comparison. It was that feeling that I fell in love with. I think they call it *awe?* That was the mistake I made. I should have chased the feeling, not the girl.

Anyway, long-story-short, she fucked me over and left. And I probably deserved it.

She even took my genuine championship belt worn by Roberto Duran. Roberto Duran! One of the greatest boxers of all times! Do you know how much it cost? Do you know how much I loved it? I would wear it to the pub sometimes and challenge people to fights. I lost it in poker games and bought it back the following mornings. It was a part of me. But nooooo she had to take it! I mean – why the fuck would she want that?

Anyway I was fucked. I had to lay off the lads and that broke my heart, even more than my wife leaving me. Some of them called me a *cunt*, others said it meant they'd lose cars, homes and wives as well. But there was nothing I could do. The only thing that stopped me from knotting up a noose was the sudden opportunity to pursue an old dream. A dream I had filed away and almost forgotten about:

Write a book.

I was good at English at school, which in itself was weird. Most future labourers in my class were just-this-side of mentally retarded. They could barely wipe their own arse without fucking it up, let alone read *Much Ado About Nothing* and understand the thing.

Even when I was running the company, a book was never far away. I kept copies of Bukowski in the truck. I had a collection of short stories by Hemingway in the site shed that I was glued to during breakfast and dinner. While the rest of the lads caught up with the footie scores, I read. I didn't *feel* above them for doing it. I just *was*.

But writing a book was what I really wanted to do. It was a stupid dream I'd had since being a kid. But when you come home late every night, either arseholed from the pub or knackered from work, it leaves little time to get it done.

But now I had nothing.

No work.

No woman.

No bollocks.

The time was right.

Only Birmingham didn't seem the best place for artistic inspiration. It seemed to have more of a genocidal impression on me, where one feels driven to self-mutilation or arson, not putting quill to papyrus. So I went online and rented a room in the first cheap countryside B&B I saw. And then I was gone. Inspiration awaited...

Goodbye cruel Birmingham, with your mortar and your whores!

What a shithole! I thought as I stumbled down the country lane, half-oiled on miniatures of G&T I'd drank on the train down. I had a travel bag thrown over my shoulder and was searching bleary-eyed for the B&B I had booked some time ago, in a far-off galaxy.

It was a rural village on the boarder of Wales and already I saw it was rife with hillbilly English and goat abusers. Some punks were riding scooters up and down the quiet street while flat-capped ex-miners shook their heads in disapproval. Almost immediately I knew that local kids would have drug problems and dental hygiene would be of little importance.

"Hello?" I called out at reception when I finally found my B&B.

"Yes. What do you want?" An angry looking woman asked me. She had the eyes of a mongoose and I was confused by her question. *What did I want? Well... to check the fuck in!*

"I have a room," I said and tried to smile.

She opened up a diary of bookings. There was only one name on the page – mine. But she placed her finger at the top of the page and slowly dragged it down until she reached me. "Ahhhhhhh yes," she groaned oddly and then slid me a rusted key. It looked as though someone had been stabbed to death with it, but I tried to ignore that.

The mongoose woman took me up to my room and left me alone. I threw my travel bag onto the bed. Inside it were some clothes, a miniscule amount of booze and some pens and paper for writing. But at that moment I felt almost completely *uninspired*. My mind was focused on an empty belly and an unsatisfied sweet-tooth.

"Come on, man!" I said to myself. *Do something!* I had paid money for this holiday. I had taken a gamble on myself with this whole writing malarkey. I couldn't waste time. I had to try!

So I went downstairs in search of mousse or something to jumpstart my creative thought. Instead I found the mongoose's husband. He was equally unpleasant and in need of some physical harm.

"Why bother?" He said when I told him about my writing idea.

His argument was stupid. "Well why bother with anything then?"

He shook his head in a way that old cunts do – with condemnation, as if their years alive somehow make them superior. It doesn't. It just makes it easier to see how very little they have achieved with their lives. I should have said:

Listen mate, you live in a hillbilly tramp village and you unhappily run a B&B, married to a mongoose. Your-opinion-is-invalid!

I chose not to insult my host. Instead I managed to bleed some information out of him.

"Go down to the lake," he said, swatting at the air.

"What's down their?"

"Water."

I left before I did something.

The old mongoose man was right. There was water down in the lake.

To use my favourite homo-curious word again, it was *beautiful* down there.

Amazingly none of the six-fingered-villagers were around, which was good news for me. I walked down an old manmade decking and looked out onto the water which lay eerily still within the mud banks. Trees lined thickly around its boarders and stood tall on ground that ran up to hills. Rays of sunlight struggled to penetrate through, but those that did danced all over the water's surface. Although I hardly saw the makings of a Penguin Classic in front of me, it was still pleasant and relaxing at the least.

I drank two more of the G&T's and felt at peace. It was a feeling I used to associate with throwing a three-and-one into the Irish washing machine, sand and cement. I had forgotten how good it felt.

After a few minutes I noticed an old man had appeared and settled down at the other end of the decking.

The decking was long, and he was sat as far away as he could. I could make out his battered jacket and beat-up baseball cap. He was sat in a deck chair and was staring corpse-like out at the lake – no fishing rod, no nothing.

Eventually I got up and walked down to him. He didn't notice me at first, or just decided to ignore. Finally he craned his neck and stared suspiciously at me. His face was deep. The wrinkles weren't merely in his flesh but carved into his soul. I could smell the heartache he carried around with him. His blood must have been like lead.

"Help you?" He asked. He was old but he still had fight in him. I noticed the way he was sizing me up.

"No, just saying *hello*," I said stupidly.

He grunted in reply. I was beyond boredom in his eyes. For him to consider me boring, meant he would have to *consider me* at all.

I decided not to make more of an arse out of myself by continuing to talk. I just stood nearby in silence. I watched as he grabbed a rucksack by his feet. His joints were stiff but determination, more from stubbornness than pride, was still within him. He pulled a flask out (like the kind Laurence of Arabia drank cholera from) and squeezed whatever was inside into his mouth.

The liquid was a funny colour, brown-like. Was it sewage?

Probably not, I decided.

When he finished taking a hit, he handed me the flask without even looking. I took it and drank. Fuck, it was sweet! It was like drinking diabetes.

I tried not to gurn the same way you would if you ate lemon. Then I handed it back. The aftertaste burnt for a while, letting me know that it was alcoholic ...thank god.

Then for some unknown reason he held the flask out in front of him and squeezed a long, steady jet into the lake. I watched the stodgy brown colour descend into the crystal clearness, slowly diluting and spreading until it vanished.

How fucking strange, I thought.

Then I remembered the G&Ts I had. Maybe he would appreciate me offering him one?

"Would you like a –,"

Before I could finish my sentence, the old timer was on his feet and swinging a perfect left-hook at my chin. Somehow I ducked and hopped back a few paces – out of his punching range.

"WHAT ARE YOU DOING? YOU MENTAL OLD FUCKER!" I shouted.

"I DON'T WANT THAT FILTH!" He growled, assembling his things, packing away the deckchair and the flask and beginning to walk away. My heart rate was up as I watched him. I was for some reason transfixed.

He was interesting. He had stories in his veins and his voice had a deep grumble, a grumble from the valleys, from lungs that had breathed coal, through teeth that had passed many drinks and been broken in many fights.

By the time my imagination calmed down he was gone – disappearing through the tree line and swallowed by shadows. It felt as though I had just seen a ghost. A violent ghost with a taste for sweet liqueur.

"Well you've found it," I heard myself say.

Found what? The rest of my brain tried to catch up.

"Your story."

The next morning I saw the mongoose husband. He was rolling a cigarette and reading the Racing Times for horses to bet on.

Is that where you first saw your wife? I was tempted to ask. But I assumed the joke wouldn't go down well.

"We have someone staying from Dorset," he said without looking at me. "The gentleman is a fan of the horses. *Are you a fan of the horses?*"

What kind of arsehole comes from Dorset? Was all I could think.

Eventually I shook my head and he winced at me in disgust.

"So I went down to the lake yesterday," I started making conversation. "I met an old bloke down there."

I saw a flicker in his face when I spoke. Like a thought had crossed his mind and he tried to hide it. "Yes, AND?"

"He seemed interesting. Do you know him?"

"That's Bram."

"Bram?"

"Yes. He's lived here as long as I can remember."

"What's his story?"

"If you want to know Bram's story, then ask Bram yourself!" He spat, turning his attention back to the Racing Times. I left the room.

For the next hour I wandered around town aimlessly. I thought about the old man and what stories he might tell. It excited me. Soon I found myself at home, scribbling words and sentences onto paper I never knew existed within me. Was I doing it? Was I actually writing? I giggled loudly and crazily to myself as I sipped warm cans of G&T.

The first thing I wrote about was his sternness. It was as though he visited the lake for a purpose, not simply recreation. The glare of his eyes. The solid planting of his feet. The clenching of his fists. And then there was his drink...

"His drink?" I said aloud, wondering what it had been.

I decided to visit the lake again the next day and bring him something similar. I would ask about the mystery liqueur at the local off-license. (I was a regular now.)

When I finished writing I was exhausted and wired at the same time.

"This'll show the bitch!" I said, dancing around the room in my socks, dizzy on gin and feeling like a weird aunt. I would have this story published. I would make millions and then I would send her death threats in the post!

Well, maybe not. I was unsure.

The next day I was still alive. So I walked to the local off-license and spoke to the Welsh woman who owned it. I enquired about a possible present for Bram.

"Oh," she said, her accent was thick. "I know just the thing!"

She waddled over to the shelf behind the counter and took down a bottle. It was dark and queer-looking but I bought it anyway. Then I crossed my fingers (and my haemorrhoids) hoping it was the right booze for Bram.

The last thing I wanted was another fist flying in my direction. I needed to befriend him. I needed to learn more about him. I needed to know it all!

Darkness descended early on the village. As dusk rolled down the valleys and into the streets and the pubs, I found myself carefully trekking through the trees, down towards the lake and the old man that knew it so well. Maybe he wouldn't be there? Doubt reverberated inside my skull. But some sixth or seventh or umpteenth sense told me *he would be*. I didn't know how. But it did.

As I pulled myself between two trees and out onto the decking, I saw Bram sat in the same spot he had been yesterday. It felt like loading up the same level on a Playstation game. It was identical. I even *felt* the same way, as I walked tipsily down the decking towards him. I had palpitations in my chest and a bottle of sugary booze swaying by my side. I felt like an idiot, but I carried on.

When I got near enough I saw him turn and look at me. Then for some reason, seemingly out-of-character, he smiled and extended a hand.

"Hello," I said and shook it.

"Evening," he said. "Sorry about yesterday."

"No worries," I sat down beside him.

He turned back to the lake and fell into his trance again. I looked him up-and-down and tried to memorise every detail for my story.

What caught my attention most was his deckchair. It must have been thirty, forty... maybe fifty years old. Burt Lancaster had probably sipped daiquiris in it. The wood was rotten to the core – almost transparent from being eaten to death by worms. The screws holding it together had rusted and grinded away to metallic dust and the fabric seat was tattered and torn to shreds, as if someone had been trying to sharpen a knife on it. Yet, like the old man sat upon it, it fought on also. I also noticed how close he placed it to the edge. When I say *close* to the edge, I mean *on* the edge. There wasn't an eight-of-an-inch between the leg of the chair and the open-air plummeting to the waters below. His legs swung happily above the peril. It made me nervous to watch.

"I brought you this," I said quickly.

Bram turned and looked at me. The harsh face he pulled at the lake dropped and he smiled again. "What is it?" He asked.

I handed him the booze and hoped he wouldn't smash it into my face.

"Very kind of you," he said. His words felt genuine.

"Do you mind if I ask you something?"

"No."

"*What's the deal with the booze?*"

"What do you mean?" He asked. He seemed honestly confused by the question. Like what he did was normal, and I was the retard for asking.

"You know, it seems quite *effeminate*," I began carefully. "And why do you throw it in the lake?"

When I finished the sentence he sighed heavily and looked away from me – back to the water. It was a short while until he replied. Until then I thought I had offended him.

"Sorry for the pause," he said and tried to laugh. Then I noticed he had been crying. "I find it hard... talking about it sometimes."

"Don't worry about it," I tried to backtrack. "I was just being nosy, it's –,"

"No, no, no. You asked me and I will tell you," he took a deep sigh as if fighting back more tears. "I grew up in this village, you see. I was born here and, if you can believe it, I was once a young man here.

(This is gold! I thought. He even spoke like a classy novel!)

"And when I was growing up here, young and stupid, I did the smartest thing I've ever done."

"What was that?"

"I fell in love. I fell in love with…" his voice broke and he suddenly barked: "Her name doesn't matter! I fell in love with the best girl this village has ever produced. Before, since, past, present, future, doesn't matter! She was the best! You might ask *how can I know that for a fact?* But trust me boy, I know!"

I watched in awe as he continued.

"We used to come here, you see," he waved a hand above the water. "We'd walk hand-in-hand down the same hill you walked down, down from the village to the lake. She was a brilliant swimmer. And I always regretted not learning myself," he paused. "I never once spent any time in the water with her…" He looked at me and I saw moisture in his eyes. I think he knew I did, so he turned away again, embarrassed. "She would swim in the lake and I would sit here and watch her." Then he grabbed up the bottle of drink I had bought him. "And this…" he pointed at it, "was her favourite. I used to buy this as a present. We'd walk down here, have a few drinks, she would swim and I would sit. Sometimes I would read but mainly…" He trailed off a bit. "Mainly I would just watch her."

"What happened?" I asked without thinking. I didn't want to know. But I had to.

"It was a normal day. She was swimming and I was watching her," Bram shook his head. "But we'd had too much to drink. I fell asleep in this fucking chair."

Some wind rolled across the lake, disrupting his story. "And?" I asked – scared at what his reply would be.

"And when I woke up…" his words drifted off and he didn't finish the sentence. He didn't need to. As cruel as it was, I think I knew how it ended.

"Drowned." He had somehow built the courage to say a word he must have detested more than any other. "They never found her…"

I didn't say anything.

There wasn't anything appropriate to say.

There wasn't anything *invented yet* that was appropriate to say.

Instead I just kept quiet and hoped the old man Bram appreciated my silence and my admiration for sharing his story. Hopefully he appreciated my company.

"I never married," he said plainly. "My wife, well, wife-to-be… she's out there."

His stony glare at the water made sense. The lake had taken his girl. The lake was her killer. Yet she was still out there somewhere. It was her final resting place. His look was one of both hatred and desire.

My own eyes began to dampen. I couldn't tell if it was from the gin, the wind or the rawest story of heart break I had ever heard. When I came to my senses Bram was deep in trance and dead to the world. Suddenly I felt like an intruder, interfering on a private moment between him and his sweetheart. I decided to leave the two lovers alone.

"Goodnight," I said as I stood.

"I've got something for you too," he said and started rummaging in his bag.

After a few moments he pulled out a four-pack of G&T's. He had remembered.

"Thank you," I said. He smiled at me. Then I took the gins and started walking back to the village. On the way up the hill I drank one of them, and then another, and then I started a third and sat down on a tree stump. What a story! I thought to myself, shuddering at the thought of putting it on paper and maybe getting it published.

Then again... another voice said. *This poor man and his heartbreak... He trusted you and opened-up to you... are you really going to use him like this?*

"Ah, shut up!" I shouted. "I deserve this!"

Halfway up the hill it started to rain. The track became slippy and dangerous. At one point I lost my footing and fell over a tree root. The root saved me from falling but it also twisted my ankle. I screamed out in pain, cursing the Welsh night.

It took me fifteen minutes to get back standing again and then another hour to get up the hill. When I got back to the B&B I was soaking wet, freezing and my ankle had swollen to the size of a melon. The mongooses, in a rare moment of empathy, summoned a doctor. He said I had sprained it and put me to bed with my foot elevated. He told me to keep off it for a couple of days. I obliged.

Over the next two days I wrote furiously. I came up with back stories, beautiful scenes and everything else in between. I even considered keeping his name as Bram if he agreed. When my foot was better I would visit him one final time and let him know my plans. I was scared he would be against it, but in reality he had no choice.

It took me a lifetime to walk down the hill with a bad foot, but I made it in the end. Yet when I stepped out onto the decking I saw no sign of him. Bram had vanished. I thought it was strange. Maybe he was late? Maybe I had just missed him, or he would come later? I didn't fancy scaling the hill again, so I walked down the decking anyway.

At first, I didn't notice what was bobbing in the water where he used to sit.

Something caught my attention and I craned over to see:

The remains of an old chair were lapping gently against the decking. There was a flask and a rucksack and a baseball cap too. I knew straight away what had happened.

"NO! NO! NO!" I cursed the lake.

My breath was stolen away.

I started whacking the decking with my crutch in a frenzy.

I had only just met him!

...and what was I doing?

I WAS GOING TO USE HIM!

I WAS GOING TO USE HIM FOR A STORY!

WHAT KIND OF SCUM WAS I?

"You could have helped him! You could have been a friend and helped him!"

The truth however became clearer and I shook my head. "No, you couldn't have," I told myself. "He wanted it…"

She had been waiting for him.

He had visited the lake every day and every day he put his chair purposefully close to the edge, waiting and willing for it to break, so he, Bram, who couldn't swim, and was withered with age and grief, could plunge downwards towards her again. Who knew how many years? How many visits? How many hundreds of thousands of hours had he sat there, waiting for sweet release?

I felt sad.

And then eventually I didn't.

There was something lovely about it, in a dark, cruel way. They were together again. He had found peace in death that had eluded him in life. I was glad I had met him.

Immediately I went back to my room at the B&B. I collected the pages, took them outside and burnt them. I would return to Birmingham. I'd start the business again. I wouldn't let that bitch win.

"What do you think you are doing?" The mongooses asked me, enquiring about the arson.

"Oh fuck off!" I finally cut into them. I couldn't be bothered to explain. Nobody was worthy of Bram's story.

And a secret love should stay secret. Forever and ever.

Wait then...

Hang on a minute...

STOP READING!

The Firs

Tommy Hughes called me early in the morning and I must have been drunk because I answered. Normally I wouldn't have. I hated the little piece of shit and I hadn't realised it was a Sunday when I slid *answer* across the phone screen. I hadn't showered in two days. I didn't on weekends. Most Fridays I bought a crate of lager, two bottles of Stolichnaya and an eight ball of cocaine. This, along with my Britpop vinyl, saw me through to Sunday.

"What?" I coughed my first word in two days.

"Come The Firs," he said and hung up on me.

Cunt. I looked wearily at the phone. I was amazed it still worked. Only last week I had dropped it down a stairwell chasing a crack dealer up a block of flats. The phone survived but he didn't. He cried before I threw him off the roof. His tears didn't affect me. He pissed his pants too and for some reason tried to show me a picture of his kid, like I cared. I did it anyway. That's what I was being paid to do. He was number three.

The Firs was the estate's local pub. Tommy Hughes ran a small crew from there that controlled the crime on the estate. He inherited me off his older brother – Martin. I only hung around Martin to sate my drug addiction and compulsion to commit violence. And he kept me close, even referring to me as a *friend* several times, but I didn't understand the word or concept. I hated Martin Hughes too, and in reality I think he only kept me close because he was scared of me. Everyone on the estate fears me, from the hardmen in the pubs to the grannies at the bus stops.

When Martin Hughes got shotgunned to death by a gypsy in 2015 it should have been me who took control of The Firs firm, but I was a drug addict and an alcoholic and too stupid. So it fell to his younger, crueller, cock-eyed brother Thomas. Thomas was the butt of all the jokes when Martin was top dog. He didn't like me. He didn't like me because I spoke dirt about his dead brother and because I didn't call him *Hughesy*. Everyone called Martin *Hughesy* instead of Martin and I think Tommy wanted to inherit the name and the connotations that went along with it. He may have done. But not with me. And I didn't refuse to do it out of loyalty to Martin. Fuck Martin. I just did it to annoy Tommy.

I got up from the couch in my flat and decided I was in no rush. I finished a glass of Stolichnaya and lit a Chesterfield. *Do It Yourself* had run over on my record player so I went and turned it off. Beside it was a line of powder, racked and ready to go. Why hadn't I finished it? I asked myself. But I didn't think too long. I took the devil's dandruff up my nose and patted down my hair in the mirror. It was thick, curly and greasy and didn't fit in with the crowd in The Firs. They all tried to keep trendy, regardless of the beer guts, missing teeth and broken noses. They had quiffs and partings – fashionable cuts. I didn't bother. I only cut mine when it started getting in my eyes when I fought. Then I pulled the leather jacket on – another *no no* I ignored. I had taken the jacket off a bouncer on Broad Street back when I was a kid. A big biker cunt used to run the door. Everyone was scared of him. Until the night I put a Carling glass in his face and broke his hand with my boot. He never came back after that. And so, the stories about me started...

There was a plastic bag hanging from the outside handle of my door. In it were some ready meals, microwavable burgers and other shit. It was from the young girl next door. For some reason she bought me this stuff. Her dad fucked off when she was young or something. I threw the bag inside and remembered the time she left her necklace in it by accident and I gave it back to her. I regretted not stealing it.

"Oh, all right Michael?" Ed the owner of the pub (on paper anyway) said when he saw me.

I nodded and walked past him, up to the bar and saw his daughter quickly fumbling to pour me a beer before I had to ask. I stood still and watched her, breathing down my nose at her. Every so often her eyes would flicker up to see if I was still watching. Her hand was shaking holding the glass and lager fizzed up at the bottom. I didn't pay. She didn't ask. Then I drank.

"Morning, Mick," Big Roy said when he saw me.

The guys called me Mick, among *other things.* But they only chatted shit behind my back. None of them had the bottle to say anything to my face. I was only five-eleven, but I was thickly built and evil. You can't beat evil.

Big Roy was a big idiot and I hated him. He spoke to me every so often but only when other people were around. One, so they could see him talking to me. And two, so people were nearby in case I kicked-off and tried to kill him, like I had done once before. He was drunk one weekend and got a little too friendly. He spilt some beer on my sleeve and didn't apologise, so I punched him on the nose in front of everybody. He went red in the face and walked out of the pub. A few of the lads told me that Tommy wasn't happy about it. But I didn't care.

"Hughesy wants to see you. He's in the back," Big Roy eventually said when he realised I wasn't going to say *hello* or acknowledge him at all.

I nodded and took a few glugs of Carling. I'm sure everyone could smell the drugs sweating out of me and the vodka on my breath and pores. But I didn't care. I was what I was.

"Where've you been?" Tommy said when he saw me shuffling towards his table. He always sat at the back of the pub, facing the door and he always had a few roid-head bodybuilders on either side. You know the kind... tattoos on the face, t-shirts too small, lots of jewellery and lots of glares but not much bite. You can't build muscles on your chin. No bottle.

"I'm here, ent I?" I said, glugging the Carling again and putting it down on his table.

"Come with me," he said, getting up and making his way out the fire exit. His henchmen followed, and I followed them.

I had a claw-hammer under my jacket, hanging from a leather holster I made myself. And if that failed, I had a kukri knife taped to my calf. The knife came in handy if I was jumped or knocked to the ground. The once I got surprised in an alleyway by a gang of speed dealers. They sucker-punched me and knocked me to the ground but I carved their legs up good with the kukri. It saved me that day.

Outside the fresh air made me feel sick. The light burnt my eyes and I half expected to get landed-on in the bin yard. There could have been a mob waiting for me, but there wasn't. Tommy was stood still, looking slightly nervous and still holding his rum-and-coke. His roid-heads carried on glaring.

"This," he said and pointed to something lying among the bin bags. It took me a moment to realise what it was. It was the body of a girl. She must have been no more than seventeen years old. I could only guess the age from her body, because there wasn't anything left of her face.

"Why are you showing me this?" I glared at Tommy.

"Who is she?" He asked.

"How the fuck should I know?"

"So you don't know anything about this?"

"You trying to say I did this?" I hissed through pursed lips.

The claw-hammer was waiting for me – eager. It was a dead-end behind them. I'd have to crack Tommy first and hope it killed him. Then I'd pull the kukri and tear into the other two, cut them to pieces and fuck off. It was tempting. But I was getting old now. Old and hung-over and I didn't have the energy, so I let it pass.

"This is Hannah Laki," Tommy said and took a cigarette off one of his monkeys. The name was familiar but not quite enough, so I shrugged and waited for him to continue. "Someone's fucked her and killed her."

"I can see that. What's it got to do with me?"

"The word-on-the-street is *you* used to shag her."

He was acting brave as he puffed on his fag.

I thought for a moment. I couldn't remember. I'd been dead drunk for most of the week, well, for most of my life. (Pretty badly the past two years.) The last fortnight was a complete blur. Usually I didn't drink at work, but I had done. I'd also had a few days off after I dealt with the dealer who wasn't kicking-up to Tommy. All of it melted into one hazy mess. Had I shagged a Hannah Laki? Recently or ever? "I might have done," I said. "But this is fuck all to do with me."

"The coppers don't know about it and we're keeping it that way. We don't want the murder squad sniffing around the pub. Understand?"

I nodded.

"You two help Mick clean this up," he said to the monkeys.

"Oi, wait a fucking minute!" I followed him towards the fire exit and grabbed him by the arm. He turned and looked at me. He was begging me to hold on, begging me to do something more so he could finally get rid of me. He never quite had the clout to take me out. The other firms liked me too much. But of course, if I did something stupid like lose my temper then he could – self-defence.

"Take your hand off me," he pulled away.

I could have held onto the scrawny cunt all day, but I thought it was probably best to let him think he was strong enough to pull free. "Now do as you're fucking told and get rid of it."

"It's my weekend. I –,"

"Just get it done."

He waved his hand dismissingly in the air and slammed the fire exit door behind him. I should have broken his fucking hand.

I turned to the other two. They were still glaring at me. My fuse was going. Old or not, hung-over or not, when my fuse went, I was a killer.

"You better look somewhere else," I said.

And they did.

Dumb and dumber went to get a Renault van to take the body away in. I stayed and waited with it, minding the door and smoking cigarettes. For the life of me I couldn't remember a Hannah Laki. But I did feel an unusual empathy when I looked at the lifeless lump among the bagged-up scraps of food and dirty mop heads. She'd had a good body, too good for such a place. Someone had seen it and wanted it, someone who wouldn't be able to get it without force. So they'd *taken it* – and in the worst possible way.

Her face was smashed apart. It had all rose up in swelling so you couldn't tell what-was-what. The cheeks had ballooned with blood, along with the forehead, all merging together. Her lips had been burst open and her nose was flattened into her skull. This mess was all obscured behind a ragged tangle of once pretty brunette hair. But even that was half ripped out and clumpy with dried blood. I noticed rings were still on her fingers and a necklace still around her purple throat. She hadn't been robbed. This was something else entirely. Only an animal, I decided. Only a sick animal could have done such a thing.

But you are an animal...

"Yes, I know!" I said aloud to some lingering conscience. "I am evil and mean. But I've never done anything like this!"

But you have killed three people...

I sighed.

I was a hypocrite.

I killed my first when I was eighteen. I was drunk on stolen whiskey and part of a gang of young thugs; me and Martin Hughes, Larry Sparks, Billy Tracey, a lot of people now dead or serving double figures. We went to brawl with another gang in Sparkhill park. I remember seeing the lights of cigarettes in the dark distance. I could smell murder in the cold air. When we fought, we fought hard. It was ridiculous really. It was too dark. We couldn't see who-was-who.

As with most incidents of violence in my life, I was too drunk to remember it entirely, but I can remember the look on the boy's face when I plunged the bayonet into his neck. It didn't seem real. There wasn't any sound or spurt of blood or anything. It just went in. He went down. We ran. He died. I never did pay for that one.

The second was the one I paid for most. I'd been up for three days on the best coke I'd ever had. It made my entire face numb when I pulled it up my nose. Three days had felt like three hours. I was out with Martin Hughes and Billy Tracey, the mad Irishman. It was match-day in Birmingham. I didn't care much for the footie, but I enjoyed the violence that went along with it. It was about ten in the morning – early for some – late for me. We ran into some away-fans in the city centre. Billy said something, they said something else and before long it was all kicking off. Tables were flying. Glasses were breaking. People were screaming. And I whacked an away-fan on the chin, hard. He went spark out and as he fell, managed to sink his temple into the corner of the bar. His head went into it and the cunt died. It was all on CCTV. My saving grace from a life sentence was the lad's priors for football violence and the fact he had cocaine in his system too. Who knows, maybe we could have been friends in another life?

I spent five years in prison for that. Most people would learn from it. But I didn't. I didn't want to.

And the third killing was the week before. Tommy Hughes gave the order, so I had to do it.

I think he secretly wanted to have some dirt on me forever, but I didn't care. I was skint and needed money for vodka and coke.

I'd seen the crack dealer around. I recognised him but that didn't matter. He wasn't a mate. I don't have mates. When he saw me coming he must have seen the devil in my face because he ran with more fear than I've ever seen.

They returned with the Renault van and a roll of polythene. Without a word they hopped out and we put on gloves. Then I spread a few meters of black polythene out in the bin yard.

"Lift her," I said quickly. (At least their DNA would be on her and not mine if she was found.)

The two monkeys did as they were told, and I took one last glance at the girl before black plastic fell over her body. We rolled her up tightly and put her in the back of the van.

"What does Tommy want us to do with her?" I asked.

The monkeys grunted at each other.

"Who?" Monkey one asked.

"Tommy Hughes! What does he want us to do?" I shouted.

"He said bury her. There's a hole already dug."

"You drive," I said and went to climb into the back.

"No – wait!" Monkey two said, glancing at his comrade nervously.

I paused. "What?"

They held each other's stare for a moment. They were nervous about something, something they couldn't talk about in front of me. Eventually the first one looked over. "You drive Mick, yeah?" He stuttered.

At that moment it hit me. I sussed it. The whole situation made itself clear. I knew what they were doing. Tommy really was a dumb cunt, putting two mongols in charge of such a task. He really did underestimate me. Either way, I nodded and walked around to the driver's side. Then I got in and started it up.

We drove to Earlswood, the countryside just outside of Birmingham. I didn't ask where we were going. The monkeys just shouted directions and I followed.

They wanted me to drive so I couldn't pull any weapons on them. I was up for slaughter. Tommy Hughes had finally grown the bollocks to give the order. I hadn't seen it coming, but now I knew their plan. They would be burying me along with Hannah Laki.

I turned right up a dirt road. We bumped past a derelict barn with an asbestos roof and deeper into some trees. I knew a family of gypos that lived nearby. They probably owned the place and were being paid handsomely for my burial plot.

Through the trees I caught site of a yellow digger. I drove up to it and saw a freshly dug hole. No one else was around.

While the monkeys sweated, I jumped out the van and peered timidly down into it. It was about seven foot deep. The blue clay was wet and dropping off the walls and old tree roots hung in like nooses. It was unappealing. I decided it was not where I wanted to live out the rest of eternity.

The fourth and fifth murders I committed took place on an abandoned farm in Earlswood...

I didn't know their names and I didn't care much for them.

While Monkey one opened the van door, I put the claw-end of my hammer through the back of his skull and into his brain. He dropped like a bag of shit and was dead before he hit the ground. Monkey two screamed in panic when he saw what I had done. He tried to pull a sawn-off from a duffle bag he was carrying, but the dozy cunt got it caught in the strap. I had the kukri off my calf and deep into his ribs before he knew what hit him.

Fair play, he struggled a bit. But I just twisted the blade, knowing it would take the fight right out of him. It did. He squealed like a pig and then his legs went, along with his bladder.

I pulled the knife back out and sat down. I watched him die in the dirt. He died beside his friend, begging hysterically for help and promising me *he wouldn't do nuffin*. His big muscles didn't help.

When he finally went, I lit a cigarette and considered burying the two of them along with the girl. I knew how to drive a digger. Then I decided *fuck it*. I'd leave as big a mess as possible for Tommy to clean up.

I had three grand in small notes hidden behind a plasterboard in a stud wall in my flat. I had unscrewed it the night before some kid plastered it for me. I put a bag in there with some emergency money – my split from an armed robbery in Wolverhampton. I was the driver.

The three grand would be enough to see me off. I'd go back to the flat, take the money and leave. There was nothing for me in Birmingham. There hadn't been for years. Probably never. I didn't even feel the compulsion to murder Tommy Hughes. Maybe if this had happened years ago, I would have. I was crazier then. But now I was older. I was thirty-one. Fifteen years of head injuries and substance abuse had sedated me. All I wanted to do now was kill myself with drugs, in a flat, alone. Vendettas required too much energy.

I was unusually nervous at the bottom of the Edward Gein flats. It wasn't fear of death. It was fear of letting that little dipshit Tommy Hughes *win*. If he caught me and killed me then he won, and I couldn't live with that (...literally).

I took the lift up to my floor and tried not to inhale the smell of urine and body-odour that clung to the walls. At a punt, I'd say Tommy was just now finding out what happened. The monkeys were probably supposed to call him after murdering me, and my flat would be the first place he'd check.

Luckily there was no sign of anyone around and my door hadn't been messed with, so there weren't any *uninvited guests* inside. I slid the key into the lock. I had to be quick. I didn't have a lot of time. The Firs was only a five-minute walk from my flat.

As I pushed the door open, I saw a shadow fall over it from behind.

Someone was behind me.

I turned quickly, reaching for the kukri.

But it was the woman from across the hall.

"I'm sorry to bother you, Mr Swaine," she said.

She was nice enough, but I didn't have time to talk. I never did. She was always in a dressing gown, and when I saw her outside the flats she walked with a cane. I think she was ill and her daughter looked after her. Her daughter was the girl who brought me food every so often.

"I'm in a rush," I said as kindly as I could.

"Oh, I'm sorry. But you haven't seen my daughter, have you?"

"No."

"It's just she hasn't been home since last night and –,"

"No I haven't," I stepped inside and shut the door.

I walked quickly to the stud wall in the living room and put my boot through the plasterboard. I fell to my knees and started digging around. For a second I thought it was gone, but then I felt the strings on the bag and smiled. The cash was still inside. Now I could make a move. But something was on my brain, poking me, annoying me, riling me. What was it? I had missed something. I was sure. But what? Was it Celtic spite niggling at me to go after Tommy? No. It was the image of that girl. For some reason I was going soft. I'd seen plenty of dead people before, but that girl from the bin yard, the one who was now slowly decomposing in a shallow grave in Earlswood, was carved into my mind's eye. I didn't understand. I'd seen much worse. I'd watched Larry Sparks rape a prostitute in Amsterdam on his stag weekend. He battered her so badly she probably never recovered. Seeing that didn't affect me. I just drank beer and fretted over the next gram. But this dead girl did... WHY, MICHAEL? I shouted at myself. Then my brain paused. The image of that necklace she had on. It was a medallion. A Saint Jude medallion.

"Hang on..." I said.

A phantom pulled the life from my lungs.

I dropped the cash to the ground. Tenners went flying everywhere but I didn't care.

Instead I rushed to the door. I threw it open and banged on the woman's flat across the hall.

I had seen that Saint Jude medallion before. I had found it. Amongst some shopping that had been left for me.

Eventually the door opened and she wearily looked up at me.

"Oh, Mr Swaine?" She seemed confused.

"What's your girl's name?" I asked quickly.

She looked vacantly at me. "I don't understand?"

"What's your girl's name?" I asked again. I must have sounded insane.

"Do you mean Hannah?"

And with that, my fate was sealed.

The Firs was unusually packed as I watched it from the darkness. I was stood in the alleyway between the shop and launderette, smoking a Chesterfield and meditating on my own demise.

There it was –

Hell.

It was waiting just beyond the doors of the pub, past the smoking chavs and inside. Tommy and his goons were in there. I'd be the topic of conversation. The one man they wanted to *see* more than any other. They would gladly send me to the hell I deserved, and they wouldn't do it quickly.

I could have taken the cash and done a runner, but some epiphany had taken place in the piss-stinking hallways of that rundown flat.

The girl didn't deserve that, I'd said to myself.

I saw images in my head, of Tommy or Big Roy or any of those cunts, sticking their dicks inside her before she was bludgeoned and strangled to death.

A lot of people don't deserve what happens to them. A lot of people didn't deserve *what I* did to them. But the girl Hannah – she was young, sweet and innocent. What they had done was beyond anything else. She had been kind to me – me, an evil cunt – and my worthless mortality was the least I could offer in repayment.

I didn't tell her mother. I thought it was a merciful act. In the past I'd always thought the unknown was more torturous than cruel truth – the never-ending *what ifs*. But that sickly woman didn't need to hear how her only child met her end. It was better that she lived in hope. Hope that maybe Hannah found a nice bloke who took her away from all the shit.

I had the sawn-off under my leather jacket. I'd checked the barrels and both were loaded. Two blasts at the door would cover most of the pub, send people running and ensure no one followed. But I didn't want that. Firstly, I wanted to make sure Tommy Hughes was dead. And secondly, I didn't want to walk out of there.

All my life I'd never found any purpose or reason to be a good man. Now, in accordance with my own twisted ethics, I had. I could go out doing something good and maybe that would make up, if only somewhat, for the pain and the suffering I had caused since I was a kid.

Earlier I had sneaked around the back of The Firs and blockaded the fire exit shut. There was no chance anyone could escape.

Since then I had been standing in the darkness for about an hour, chain smoking and trying not to fear death. I knew Tommy was in there. I was just trying to build the courage to go in and *do it*.

"Take it," I kept saying to myself. "Take it."

Take the first step.

The next step will follow.

That'll be it.

The rest will be urban folklore forever. At least until they knock the flats down and let the ghosts rest.

I took it.

And sure enough, the next step followed.

The lads smoking at the door didn't recognise me. They weren't in the firm and they didn't know what was going on.

Inside the pub I felt familiar warmth blow over my face. The hum of activity buzzed in my stomach and I craved a drink or a line, something to chill my nerves and make sure everything went as beautifully chaotic as it was supposed to.

Big Roy was at the bar with a couple of other blokes. I recognised their faces but didn't know their names. He saw me and stopped talking. Then he turned away, trying to act as though he hadn't noticed me.

"Shit," I lost my nerve and walked across to the bar. I needed something quick and something strong. I was a coward after all. "Vodka," I said to Ed the owner, he nodded and fixed me one quickly. All the while I felt eyes on me, more and more eyes, from everywhere, watching.

I slammed the double. Then I walked across to the juke box. In the reflection of the greasy glass, figures were standing and edging forwards. Maybe twenty of them.

There was a price on my head. They all wanted the money. They all wanted the glory.

I fumbled with some change in my pocket and tried to pick a song for my funeral.

What did I want to go out to?

My mind was too fucked-up to think. So I just picked a song I'd been whistling all day. It was an old favourite:

Blinded By The Sun.

The music started and I walked into the centre of the bar.

I noticed the door had been blocked by a few men. But that didn't matter.

I pulled out the sawn-off.

I called Tommy's name.

Then I put a shell through the ceiling.

Screams rang out, mainly from a table of women drinking wine. I nodded at them and they scarpered away. The men at the door separated for a moment to let them out, and from the darkness I could still hear the echoes of their cries.

With them gone the pub was almost entirely firm. Most hands were inside jackets, grasping handles of hammers or knives or maybe even shooters. It was brewing…

From the back of the pub, where he usually sat, Tommy Hughes walked out. His face was smirking at me – which was unwise. I hated the little shit so much. He was walking into his own death and he didn't even know it. That had always been his problem – ego – he was always too concerned with his own brilliance to know when real danger slouched before him.

"Fucking hell, it's just the man I wanted to see!" He said. I didn't say anything. I just aimed the smoking barrel at his chest and watched him continue to smile. "What's the plan then, Mick? Kill me and walk off into the sunset?" Still I didn't respond. "You're a dead man."

"Why'd you kill her?" I finally asked.

I wasn't concerned with trading insults. I wanted to know why that girl had to die. Because of me? Because of Tommy? Because of all us scumbags that ruined the estate?

He shrugged, and I felt my trigger-finger itch.

"Because I could," he smirked. A low murmur of laughter rose around the pub. Laughter from men who had had *their turn* on Hannah as well. "It was an excuse to get rid of you. No one would doubt that you did it," I aimed the barrel a little higher. "But I don't need an excuse now. Not after what you did to Mike and Stu," I guessed they were the monkeys I butchered.

"You didn't have to fucking do it," I snarled through gritted teeth. "You could have done me. No problem. She had fuck all to do with it."

"Oh who gives a shit?" Tommy spat. "She was just some fucking slut! After tonight no one will know. She disappeared. You disappeared. Life goes on without you!"

I was almost ready. I started breathing heavily.

I didn't deserve mercy from God, but I begged for it anyway.

"Are you finished with this performance?" He carried on. Tommy never did know when to shut-the-fuck-up. "You're not going to do anything. We all know that. You haven't got the fucking bottle. My brother Martin always said..." I shut my eyes and raised the barrel to head height. "Michael Swaine doesn't have any bottle..."

Blinded By The Sun was building up to the chorus.

I decided now was as good a time as any.

My funeral was in full swing – only I was late to it.

I opened my eyes.

Tommy was still there, arms extended and cursing my name.

The rest of the pub was on their feet, weapons drawn, edging nearer to me.

I was surrounded. I had one barrel. One wasted life. One last chance for a slither of redemption.

TAKE IT, MICK!

I let the barrel go and watched Tommy's head explode.

And then the pub tore me to shreds.

Just Me and My Hunger

Dear friend,

I live alone with my hunger. Sometimes I speak to the old man who lives underneath the bed. Sometimes he speaks back. Sometimes I don't think he exists. I have a couple of dogs I breed. I keep them in the loft. They don't breed too well now though. They're sixth generation inbred. The pups don't live too long. But they live long enough for me to feed that hunger. I painted the windows black but the sun has burnt some of the paint off. This scares me. I don't want to look outside because the hunger doesn't know how to control itself and I don't know how to control it. I order food on the internet and the men bring it up the stairs and leave it at the door. I have a long sheet nailed to the inside of the door frame. I open the door from behind the sheet and push it out into the hall until I see the food beneath it. The sheet is black and thick. I cannot allow myself to see the hall in case I see somebody. I've never seen anybody in the hall. But if I ever did then something bad might happen. Most days I try to sleep. I try to sleep at day and at night to stop the hunger from talking to me. But sometimes the hunger comes for me in my dreams. The hunger never stops. It is in me. It always was. It always will be. The hunger is me. I am hunger. I am hungry for the worst things. The old man talks to me about the hunger. He says he had it to. He said the hunger wanted to eat and he tried to stop it, so then the hunger ate him instead. I think the hunger is eating me. I think maybe it already has. I don't know. I don't know anything anymore. All I know is fear. I fear the outdoors. I fear the inside. I fear the old man who might or might not exist and I fear myself. I fear my thoughts and fear what I might do. I don't understand where the thoughts come from. I don't want to think them. They just appear in my head and won't leave me alone. They won't leave me alone until I do what they want. Something bad must have happened to me. Or maybe it didn't. Maybe I was just born with these desires and with no way of controlling them. There is money in my bank account for rent and bills and food. I don't know how the money got there. I think maybe I had a job at one time, at one point in my life. I think maybe I had savings or retired or inherited money off a wealthy parent. I can't remember anything anymore. I think I must have chosen to lock myself away to stop me from doing bad things. Now I just exist in a nameless, shapeless void. I am drowning in the shadow of a cavern at the bottom of the ocean. That is my home. I am drowning but I never drown. Dying. I am dying forever. Not alive anymore. Not dead yet. Just dying for eternity. My name is lost. Maybe the walls know my name and my story. I don't know anymore. I don't know my age. I don't know my face. I don't have mirrors. But if I did have mirrors only a stranger would be staring back. And maybe the old man would be behind me, looking back too. The idea scares me. So I smashed all the mirrors a long time ago. I think I did. I'm not sure. The lights turn themselves off. I don't like the dark. I don't know what is in it. But when I turn a light on and leave a room, it is switched off when I return. It is endless. The darkness never stops chasing me. In me. Around me. In my flat. It is always there. Only a step away. One room away. One thought away. The walls make sounds. I used to think it was the rats talking to me from within them. The old man says the noises are from the neighbours. He says the neighbours would sate my hunger. I don't believe the old man. I think he lies. I think he doesn't exist. (But don't tell him that because it makes him angry.) And when he gets angry all the lights turn off. I think the noises in the walls are from something else. Not from the neighbours and not from the rats. But something else that got stuffed into the cavities between the damp, the rodent faeces and the insulation a long time ago. Maybe I stuffed those things in there. The things that smell. The things that talk to me. Or maybe I didn't. I don't know. I need to stop talking now. I can hear the old man calling me. The light bulb above me is going dim. I will talk to you again. I like to pretend I have a friend.

Dear friend,

I saw her again today. I can't remember the first time I saw her. I have no concept of time. Days burn into whatever weeks are, years, months. They go by. And they take me with them. The cracks in the black paint on the windows were to blame. I thought the sun did that. But they look more and more like claw marks. Maybe I clawed them out, in desperation, in my sleep. But I don't sleep. I think the old man did it. He wanted me to see her. And I did. She was walking past the flat without any knowledge of my existence or of my thoughts. She couldn't feel my gaze run up her body and she couldn't feel whatever I felt inside of me. Every time she passes the window, back and forth, I am there. I have learnt. I find myself there, face pressed against the glass. Breath and condensation and eyes. I know her face. I know her brown hair. The old man watches her with me sometimes. He says things about her that make me cry. So I hide up in the loft and play with my puppies until I feel better. Then I clean up. She would release me from my prison. I am sure she would. She would love me. Maybe she would live here with me and ask the old man to leave. That thought makes me happy. But whenever I think about it the lights turn themselves off. And then I scream and wail. I hate my hell. I hate the old man and I hate me. But I love love love her. She is my angel with no name.

Dear friend,

Some time ago another man came to my flat. He knocked on the door and shouted. He said I owed money. I didn't know him. He came back again and again. It started with an envelope under the door. Demands and a bill. I ignored it. I ignore everything from outside the door. Things outside the door might lure me. And I cannot be lured. But that shouting man kept coming back. Banging. Shouting. Demanding. I cried to the old man and he told me I was a disgrace. He told me to open the door the next time he came back. I can't remember if I did. I can't remember if he came back or not. But the old man smiles and mentions the shouting man sometimes. I think he did something. Or I did something. There are gouges in the plaster on the walls. Chunks missing from door frames. I smelt bleach for days. I try not to think about the shouting man or what might have happened. But the old man knows it upsets me. He likes to upset me. So he mentions it. I am so pathetic. I hate myself. I wish I had the strength to tell him to leave. I wish I had the strength to walk out of the door. But I am scared. I am weak. I am a weak man who plays with puppies and fears everything.

Dear friend,

She didn't walk by today. I waited. I might have missed her. I am stupid and ugly. I might have missed her because I'm stupid. But I never miss her. Maybe she was ill today. Maybe she contracted some sort of virus and had to stay in bed, in her flat. I wonder if she has an old man in her flat who tells her things she doesn't want to hear? Who smiles at her from the corners of rooms? Who follows her everywhere she goes? I doubt it. I am special in my suffering. I waited by the window for hours, maybe days. She didn't pass by. It made me angry. I felt angry and full of hatred. Indiscriminate uncontrollable rage. So I dragged my nails down the inside of my arms. I wanted to tear my skin open and drag the veins out. I could bleed then. I could remind myself I am human. I am a man and I am allowed to be angry and sad. I am not a ghost. I am not dead. This is not hell. But curls of skin built up under the nails and then I couldn't do it anymore. I tasted blood in my mouth. My gums were bleeding. So I spat blood onto the wall and drew a picture. The old man liked the picture. I think maybe it was of her. Maybe it was of me. A self-portrait. I didn't know. But the pain and the blood helped. Apart from lust, pain is all I can feel. But my lust for her, in her absence, is terrifying.

Dear friend,

The puppies are dying. I found out when I hid in the loft today. The old man was talking about his hunger again. It scared me. He was telling his stories. What he did. This time to an old lady. So I corkscrewed my thumbs into my ears and screamed so I didn't have to hear. The light went off in the loft, so I screamed even more. When it came back on, I saw the puppies were dying. The litters are getting smaller and smaller. This will be the last one. They are fucking their siblings too much. The newest litter was only three. One was born dead. One was overly disfigured. (I played with that one first because I knew it would be first to go.) And the final one. The only one. Was crumpled in a heap of fur and puss, breathing from somewhere, pining for a mother that was long dead. I cried by the puppy. It was the only friend I had. Below me in the flat the old man was laughing. His laugh echoed. It carried. Like disease. The puppy is dead now. I played with it too rough. I am alone now. Truly alone. I need her.

Dear friend,

I awoke stood by the wall today. I was punching, punching, punching. My knuckles were twisted and swollen and the wall was ready to cave in. Why was I doing this? Why was I here? I couldn't remember, so I stopped and looked around. The old man was not there. There was a letter on the floor by the window. I tried to read it, but my eyes kept flickering at the gap in the black paint. I was waiting for her. The letter was from the police. It said they visited the night before, or at least tried to. I had obviously not answered. It was a noise complaint. Maybe from punching the walls. Maybe from screaming when the old man told me that story. His story was about an old lady who lived alone. He had broken into her house during the night. He told me he made himself a sandwich before he went up the stairs and into her room. I tried to paper cut myself with the letter but I couldn't, so I screwed it up and tried to eat it. I will punch the wall again later. There is no sign of her again. Maybe she is dead. Maybe she is playing with the puppies in heaven. All of them are waiting for me. And I am still here, enclosed between the walls I am trying to break down. Tormented and dead. I should die maybe. I have been thinking about dying. How could I do it? The fall from the window is not high enough. I would only break bones and be taken away. There are no knives or rope in the flat. I could try to chew through an electric cable or just gnaw my wrists. Until dark I stood by the window and waited for her. She didn't go by. So I went to the walls and started punching them again. My knuckles hurt. They are all broken. But I like the pain. So I carried on until there was a big hole in it. Then I looked inside. Something was stuffed in the wall. I prodded it. It felt like uncooked meat. It smelt. So I filled the hole back up and started circling the flat. I walked with my back to the wall. Along the border. The perimeter. Nothing could jump out. Nothing could creep up behind me. No scares. No ghosts. No demons. No old man. The old man? I have not seen the old man in some time. I call out to him while I write this. He does not reply. I rush around the flat but cannot see him. I turn around, spinning, again and again until I collapse and feel feint. He likes to stand behind me and whisper. Or just stand behind me and watch. But I cannot see him. I haven't seen him for a long time. Maybe he has gone. Maybe he has moved out. Maybe I have just imagined him. For some reason I miss him. I'm up in the loft now, swatting away the flies that are eating the dead puppy's eyeballs. I am alone now. I am crying out for someone. I am crying out for misery.

Dear friend,

My hunger is terrible now. Unbearable. No man, god or creature can tolerate this. God? Maybe I am god. Maybe this is my heaven and I am looking down on creation through the cracks in the black paint. But where is the old man? He has left me now. He is chewing on the mind of another, maybe in my neighbour's flat. Or maybe I am the old man. Maybe I have lived in this flat far longer than I know. Maybe the things he did, I did. Maybe they are what torture me. She will answer my questions. She will give me back my sanity. I stand by the window and claw at the paint more and more. Waiting and waiting until I see her once again. My eyes are burning red with fatigue and hunger. But they still work. AND THEN SHE APPEARS... My beautiful. My destiny. Walking. Naïve. She awaits me below. This hunger can no longer be resisted. I must bid farewell to the flat. I must leave. I am frightened but excited. I go to the door now. The old man holds it for me and we shake hands. I need to finish what I am writing. Wish me luck. Goodbye friend.

Story From the Concrete Footings

I was in charge of concrete. I was working at Holloway Circus in the city centre. It was a crazy place. One night a car-full of dipshits tore themselves apart in a nearby tunnel underpass. The local news said six people were in the car when it crashed, doing one-hundred on the wrong side of the road. One of the labourers from the site had seen the crash and took pictures on his phone. He showed me one...

A white Air Max trainer was wedged in the roof of the tunnel and a leg was hanging out of it.

"Delete that fucking thing!" I said and pushed him away.

His name was Ted Onion. "Nah mate!" He barked back, giggling. "It's HIL-AR-IOUS!" Then he craned his neck and pulled that stupid smile – waiting for me to laugh – which I didn't.

Ted Onion (or *oh-nigh-on* as he pronounced it) spent most of his days throwing and missing shovelfuls of sand at a nearby cement mixer. *Never mention the shovel!* I was warned by other trades on the site. But one time I did and it was a huge mistake. He didn't shut up about it for hours. It was made of *Idaho brass*, supposedly, and he told me he could lift steel RSJ's with it. Then again... when he found out I was a weekend golfer he also told me he could drive three-hundred yards with a putter... *And* last weekend at his nephew's baptism the priest was so drunk that Ted Onion himself had to take over and perform the ceremony. In technical talk: he was a gobshite. He was also a psychopath. He used to put WD-40 in his hair to act as gel and at work he feared anything but ground level. He had a phobia of heights, so couldn't work on scaffolding, and he also had a fear of depths, so couldn't work in footings.

When Ted Onion left me alone I went and spoke to the site manager. He was called Benny. But the lads called him *Benny The Bellend*.

"How many tons of concrete do we need?" Benny asked.

YOU'RE THE MAN WITH THE CALCULATOR! YOU TELL ME! I thought

"About thirty-six cubes," I instead replied.

"Cubes of what?"

"Concrete."

"Oh, yes, right, of course…" The Bellend started calling up whoever his supplier was. "Cubic *meters*, is it?" He asked. I wanted to say *no* just to fuck with him, but I nodded anyway.

"What size pump do you want?" I heard the voice on the other end of the phone ask.

"Thirty-six meters," The Bellend said without shame. I shook my head and walked away.

This was going to be a bollock-ache of a job! I thought to myself. I had only been at Holloway Circus for two days and it was already driving me mad.

After work I went to the pub with a few of the lads. I ordered a pint of Guinness and then went for a long, self-reflective piss. I looked at myself in the mirror and decided I had probably wasted most of my life. All of my friends were in comfortable office jobs. They had travelled the world and married nice women. But I was still stuck raking concrete and conversing with arseholes. I shrugged at myself. What else is there? I didn't know. So I went back to the Guinness.

The topic of discussion was the high-rise flats that surrounded Holloway Circus. Recently, I had been told, the local delinquents who lived there (and didn't approve of seven o' clock starts) had declared war. Residents had thrown frozen bags of peas into the site and Ted Onion was keen to show me the picture evidence on his phone. The situation had grown more serious when the same residents stole planks off nearby scaffolding and began launching them off balconies. No one had been injured yet, but there were some close calls. The local council didn't do anything because the flats were partly private-owned and the police didn't respond to calls.

"You heard about the druggies?" One of the lads, an electrician I think, asked me.

"No."

So they told me...

Not only did the high-risers throw dirty needles into the site, but the other day a madman had scaled the gate and started forcing the rusty hypodermics into the veins on his arms, desperate to find any trace of drug. The banksman to the crane shooed him away but the madman escaped with a tin of Hammerite paint.

"Pieces of shit," I muttered into the froth of the Guinness.

A few hours later I found myself alone with Ted Onion. I glanced wearily down at the full pint I still had to drink and I cursed myself for ordering it. No way could I leave without drinking it. That would be sacrilegious! But that also meant I had to talk to *him*.

"Can you keep a secret, me old mate?" He asked and then gurned that weird grin.

"Fuck no," I replied, trying to finish the Guinness quickly without vomiting.

"Ah, cum on! I want to show you something!"

Somehow, in a blur, I found myself walking behind him and smoking a cigarette. We had left the pub and began down the street. It was then that I realised it was a Tuesday night and I would have to be up and at work for seven the next morning. When I looked at my phone I saw it was nearly two. I felt depressed. Five fucking hours...

"Come here!" I heard Ted say.

I looked up and saw he had led me back to the site.

"What are we doing here?" I asked, worriedly actually, because no one (not even Ted himself) had mentioned his bird or missus or even an interest in the opposite sex.

"I want to show you something," he gurned at me.

"Well I hope it's not your cock," I said and followed him up to the gate.

He vaulted it first. And although I was sceptical, I was also very pissed, so I jumped over and descended into the dark with him. We meandered through stacks of bricks, ducked under scaffolding and walked around parked up machines. Eventually we got to the far corner of the site, right beside the cement mixer and his securely chained-up brass shovel.

I gritted my teeth at him. "If you brought me here to show me that fucking shovel again I'll –,"

"No!" Ted said and bent down. His jeans slipped and I could see the crack of his arse. "LOOK!" He said.

Oh Jesus. "Yes I've looked now Ted…" I averted my eyes. "Now can you pull up your –,"

"NO! LOOK!" He pointed at a shadow.

I couldn't see a fucking thing, so I got the torch working on my phone. It looked as though Ted Onion was pointing at a bag of dog shit, but then I looked closer. It wasn't dog shit. It was brown powder. It was a big bag of brown powder. Heroin, I guessed.

"Jesus," I said.

Ted Onion explained: "Some tit was legging it from the coppers at lunch time today. He lobbed it over!" Then he picked it up and gurned at me.

"Don't touch it, you prat! You'll get fingerprints on it!" I tried to swat it out of his hand but Ted was a big bollocks, so he kept me away with ease.

"What do you think about selling it?" He half said/half asked me.

I immediately shook my head. "You're insane. Just hand it in tomorrow and be done."

"No thank you! There's money to be made here!"

Suddenly I felt nervous. He had told me now. I was an accomplice. If...no...*WHEN* he fucked up then I could be in trouble too. I knew. And I hadn't stopped him or grassed on him. I had found myself yet another headache.

"Ted, listen to me. Hand it in tomorrow to The Bellend. He'll deal with it."

I watched him stuff it down the front of his pants and shake his head. "Not a chance, mate."

I thought for a moment. But not for too long...

"Ah, fuck you then!" I said and walked back across the site to vault the fence. I struggled for a bit because of the Guinness but eventually hauled myself, and the barrel in my stomach, over and onto the Birmingham street.

A shadowed figure was watching me from outside one of the high-rises. I held his stare for a moment but decided I was in no condition to fight. Besides, it was almost three in the morning. I had to be up in two hours.

The next morning I was a zombie at work. I only managed ninety minutes sleep and decided the other thirty wouldn't do me any good. Why bother? I asked myself, weary and sick, falling out of bed and trying to wake up with an ice cold shower.

I got dressed and went to site early. While I waited for The Bellend to arrive I stood by the gates, shaking, smoking and dying.

"Early starter?" He smiled gayly when he saw me and I forced a nod.

I went straight to the thunder-box and vomited my guts up. The smell of cigarettes was on my mouth and I could hear traffic and horns echoing from inner-city Birmingham outside. Jesus, I was in hell! I thought, only then realising my cuffs were damp from the piss-wet toilet seat. I got shakily to my feet and wiped some drool from my chin. Then I went back out into the day.

More people had arrived but there wasn't much for me to do. I had to finish digging the footings, but that was only half a day's work. The next morning concrete would arrive. It would be poured and I would have to level it out. So to kill some time I went back to the entrance and smoked again.

I was trying to build the courage to eat something. That was when I saw him. A big, burly black guy was leaving one of the high-rises and looking at me in an odd way. Yes it was aggressive. But it seemed to be aggressive for a reason. I didn't recognise the man. What the fuck had I done? I asked myself as he disappeared into traffic. Only then did it click. He was the person staring at me when I jumped the gate last night. Was he just a local maniac or something much more?

When I started working I kept the window down on the JCB. Normally I kept the cabin solitary... windows up, heated seat on, radio on. But this time I was trying to get as much oxygen possible and feel as less panicked and claustrophobic as I could.

When I finished digging the footings I gave my labourer a thumbs-up. He had been measuring the depth for me, but now that we were finished he began walking away to make us a couple of coffees.

"How d'you want your coffee?" He asked as I climbed down from the JCB.

"HE LIKES HIS COFFEE THE SAME WAY HE LIKES HIS BOYS!" Someone shouted. "BLACK AND SWEET!"

A roar of laughter went up on site.

I turned to see who it was that accused me of being a racially-inclusive-paedophile, but I couldn't see anyone. People were laughing while working and I didn't have the energy to shout anything back. When I looked back to the labourer he was still waiting for an answer.

"Actually, he was right," I shrugged.

"PEEEEEEEEDOOOOO! PEEEEEEEDOOOO!" The cretins started to chant.

I put my head in my hands and sighed.

After a sweet black boy - COFFEE! Fuck, I mean COFFEE.

After a *sweet black coffee* I was feeling better. I did a few laps of the footings to kill some time and measured the depth even though I knew it was right. Relief engulfed me. I was done for the day. There was nothing more to do until the concrete arrived the next morning.

"OI!" Someone said from behind. I sighed and awaited the next paedophile accusation, but it was Ted Onion.

"What is it?" I asked dismissingly, trying to get away.

"I need to talk to you."

"No you don't."

"I do! I do!" He shouted.

I digged him in the arm. *"Shut up!"*

"Please!" He begged.

I followed him over to the cement mixer and saw his prized brass shovel was in the dirt. This led me to believe that something must have been seriously wrong.

"Did you do what I told you?" I asked him before he could speak.

He stared blankly at me, as if lobotomised.

"Did you give The Bellend the drugs?" I explained.

He shook his head.

"Fucking idiot!" I hissed.

"I'm scared."

"You don't need to be scared," I started. "Just take them to him *now*. Tell him you just found them. He'll believe you. You'll be fine."

"It's not that," he said. "Some motherfucker has threatened me! Can you believe it?"

I raised an eyebrow and tossed what was left of my cigarette away. "*Who?*"

He began to explain to me – in *great* detail...

While he was knocking up a mix, a face had appeared between the fencing. The face had demanded his drugs back. Ted Onion, being the intellectual cat he was, tried to play dumb but somehow the face knew. It had seen him take them. I knew immediately who *the face* was. It was the big bastard from last night and this morning who had been sharking me.

"What did I tell you, you idiot?" I growled. "I told you to hand it in!"

"What can I do now? I'm in a right –,"

"HAND-IT-IN!"

"But he's going to kill me if I don't give it back!"

I sighed and lit another cigarette. The one by my feet wasn't even out yet. What could I do? I asked myself. Should I give the stupid arsehole up and rat him out to The Bellend? No, you can't do that! I said to myself. Yes you're a wanker but you're not *that much* of a wanker! The man was obviously backwards. He could get sent to fucking prison. But what else was there to do?

"He said he wants them back tonight. I have to meet him here," Ted said and put a hand on my shoulder.

I pushed him away. "Give them back then! Why're you telling me?"

"Because you're my mate. You'll help me, won't you?"

"No."

"Please."

He looked as though he was about to cry and I didn't know what else to do. Ted Onion had ruined another day for me. It had been going good, work was done and the hangover had pissed off. But now I had agreed to help a retard in a drug deal with a psychopath. Why? Why? Why?

I told him to meet at the pub later that night. We would come up with a plan and walk to the site together. Then I started on my way home in search of some sanity.

"Concrete wagon is coming at seven o' clock sharp!" Benny The Bellend said to me as I left.

I nodded. Concrete was the last thing on my mind.

I sank three Guinness's before Ted Onion turned up. He had booze on his breath as well. He was nervous and rightly so. The pair of us could be murdered by the end of the night, hospitalised or arrested in possession of an ounce of heroin – enough for a nice double figure sentence. I asked myself why I was doing it. I decided it was because of denial. I was in denial at the boredom and tedium of my own life. Concreting wasn't enough for me. I felt a failure in comparison to my friends and my brothers and everyone else. Would drug dealing put me above them? No. But it offered some excitement that my life seemed exiled from.

"I'll do the talking," I told Ted Onion.

He nodded and at a glance I saw the lump in his front pocket where the bag of smack was. I'm sure other people in the pub probably saw it too and had no idea what it was.

When the time was right I ordered two double Jameson's. We slammed them and started on our way back to the site. As I reached up to clamber over the gate I smelt cannabis and I knew our transaction partner was waiting for us. My heart was racing but I hadn't felt as alive in years, maybe ever.

There was a pause after I landed before Ted started pulling himself over. I guessed he was considering running. Maybe that would have been the smart thing to do – the *only* smart thing Ted Onion ever did – but, in Ted-Onion-fashion, he didn't do it.

"Where is he?" He asked me.

"How should I know," I said, trying to hide the chattering of my teeth as I walked deeper into the site.

What lay in wait? I asked the shadows and the voices in my brain.

After a few moments of impending terror I spotted his broad silhouette. He was stood by the cement mixer, hovering by the edge of the footings. Embers from a joint lit up his face and illuminated one menacing scowl.

What-the-fuck-are-you-doing? I asked myself, suddenly hoping this was some kind of schizophrenic delirium or masochistic dream.

As my strides dwindled into baby-steps, I eventually reached him. "Alright?" Was all I could think to say.

"Whose got it?" He asked and I noticed a lock-knife in one of his hands, joint in the other.

"He does," I said, feeling the fear radiating from Ted beside me.

The man extended one large, scarred hand in our direction and I nodded to Ted Onion. He fumbled around in his pocket like the buffoon he was, eventually pulling the bag free and shakily handing it to the man in front of him.

There was silence for a moment. All I could hear was a heartbeat. His? Mine? Ted's? Or in that moment had they all somehow synchronised?

A flash woke me up. Something silver cut through the shadows and glinted in the light of a streetlamp. I saw the blade slicing in my direction just in time. I stumbled backwards, avoiding the cut but tumbling into the footings and putting my back out.

The pain shot through me like a bullet and I winced. My eyes shut and I heard screaming and scuffling and swearing from above me. I tried to move but the shooting agony in my spine was too much.

"WHOA! WHOA!" I shouted instead, seeing nothing but a smoggy sky above the dirt. "WE GAVE YOU WHAT YOU WANTED! WHAT ARE YOU DOING?"

From somewhere beyond the footings I heard him growling:

"You two cunts! You know what would've happened to me? If Hughesy knew I'd lost his gear?"

I heard Ted scream again.

"MATE! STOP! PLEASE!" I shouted up.

"I've been shitting myself for two fucking days..." he said again, now from a different part of the footings, obviously chasing Ted to stab. "I couldn't tell anyone about it... I couldn't shift any of it... Now I'm fucked!"

Suddenly heavy oafish footsteps started to run away and all the screaming and talking stopped. There was a silence again, especially in the damp dirt of the footings. I tried to move but my back was locked up.

I bit down on my fist to stop crying out. From there I clawed at the walls, grabbing some hanging roots and pulling myself upwards, trying to ignore the pain. Then, for the first time ever since meeting him, I prayed and prayed that Ted Onion would be waiting for me. But my prayers went unanswered...

"You're mate has bailed on you," the man said, waiting and playing with his knife. I saw the white teeth of a Doberman chattering from his mouth as he glared downwards. Was this it?

"Please..." I started to beg, feeling myself sliding back down into the footings again. "There's no need for this mate... You've got what you want... I won't speak a word to anyone about it... Who can I tell? I'm not even from Birmingham... I'm gone tomorrow after work! That's the end of it! I was just trying to help him... It was *him* that took your drugs... not me! He needed help to get them back to you... I just tried to help... Please! Please don't do this!"

WHACK

I heard a soft, fleshy thud come from above me, like a hammer pounded into clay. Looking up from the blackness I saw a spew of thick, red blood jet from the man's head and down onto the dirt beside me. Then I realised what had happened. Ted Onion had buried the brass shovel into the side of his head.

His body shuddered and then collapsed into the footings beside me. For a moment I thought he was attacking, but the movements from his body were just twitches and shakes, dying signals from a soon to be dead brain. Ted Onion had killed him.

"WHAT THE FUCK HAVE YOU DONE!" I panicked, trying to get away from the convulsing corpse and up-and-out of the footings. Ted helped me and then I pushed him away.

"He was going to kill you! He was going to kill us!" He tried to explain. The blood-stained brass shovel was still swinging in his grip.

"BUT, but…" My mind was in a blur – partly from the adrenaline and partly from the Jameson's.

"I killed him," Ted Onion said.

For the first time in his life – he was right.

The next morning I was early for work again. Benny The Bellend seemed somewhat suspicious, or maybe he didn't, maybe that was just my paranoia at work.

"You really need to cut down," he said as he opened the gates beside me. I glanced and saw half a dozen fag ends, freshly smoked by my boots. I nodded and half coughed a joke at him before walking into the site.

"Concrete still on time?" I asked.

"As far as I know."

I made my way across to the footings and stood nervously on the dirt. I looked down into them, the two meter trenches that would soon be nearly filled. I remembered the night before and I remembered the day ahead.

Pallets of unopened bricks were lined up behind me. They had been ordered for the bricklayers but they wouldn't be starting until the concrete for the foundations was poured, levelled and set. No one would disturb them... or the dead body that was hidden behind them.

(After Ted Onion killed the man with the shovel, we stuffed his body behind the bricks. I had a vague plan in my head but not really. No one *really* can plan for something like what we were trying to do.)

"I think I'm in the shit," someone said, and I jumped.

I turned and saw The Bellend beside me. He was stood only six feet from the body.

"W-what? Sorry?" I stuttered, trying to recompose.

"I'm in the shit," The Bellend repeated. "We're a full six weeks behind schedule," he continued. "Head office is talking about replacing me... at least I've heard through the grapevine."

"Sorry to hear it."

"I might be able to pull it back," he turned and looked at me. "I need everything to run smooth."

I nodded and smiled. Oh boy! If only he knew just how fucking *un-smooth* things actually were.

Half an hour later the concrete wagon arrived. It backed into the site and the pump began pouring several meters at a time in different parts of the footings. I, and three labourers, walked the perimeter raking the liquid while another held a laser level staff. As the beeps slowed and then held steady, we knew the concrete was level. The Bellend watched us. Then, as planned, Ted Onion approached him and began shouting. All eyes fell on the dispute that Ted was raising. No one noticed as I went behind the bricks, dragged the body out and rolled it into the footings. But just as it splashed, my eyes met with The Bellend's. He knew. He saw. Maybe he didn't know completely but he knew that something was up. And what did he do? Nothing. The job came first.

I took a few steps forwards and watched the lifeless lump descend into grey hell, bubbling into nothing. I took a deep breath and called out:

"Double-check it here, mate!" I beckoned the man with the staff.

He walked across and lowered it in. It was a few inches out of level from when the body had plunged through. It took me a minute or so to rake it back to how it was and then the deed was done. The body settled below the concrete and for company it had mine and Ted's eternal soul. Just what had we done? I stayed for a while longer than I had to. The Bellend thanked me and told me I could leave but I didn't. I watched it beginning to set, now holding a macabre secret deep within. I wondered if anybody; children, a girlfriend or an older relative depended on the man we had killed? Ah fuck him! Another voice in my brain spoke up. He was a piece of shit drug dealer.

At one point I saw Ted Onion walking over to me but I stopped him dead in his tracks.

"Don't speak to me again, ever," I said and he nodded sadly. "Don't tell anyone about this until the day you die, understand? Forget it. It never happened. You never worked here. You never took those drugs. You never killed that man. And you never met me."

As I went to walk away he stopped me.

"I've still got them," he whispered. *"How about we… you know? Like we spoke about? Sell them?"*

After all that had happened… he still wanted to sell them.

I didn't curse at him.

I didn't punch him.

I just walked away.

A few years later I bumped into an electrician that had worked on the Holloway Circus job. We went for a drink after work and I asked him about Ted. He shook his head. He said he didn't have a clue. After Holloway Circus was completed Ted vanished. No one had heard anything off him since. Maybe he did find someone to sell the drugs to. Maybe he fucked off to the Caribbean to live the life of Riley. But something else told me that he hadn't. Something else told me that Ted Onion, most probably, was in the footings of another building somewhere else, just like the man he murdered.

Fred (Under the Bed)

She didn't see Fred watching her. She didn't see him watching as she slid a spare set of keys under the wheelie-bin. It was pissing down and she was late for drinks with friends, so instead of noticing him she fumbled with her hood and rushed across to the taxi. She hadn't seen Fred. But Fred had seen her.

As the taxi dissolved into the traffic, Fred dragged himself across the road. He weaved through standstill cars and buses and ignored the cursing or honking of horns. When he reached the bin he first checked inside for scraps of food, but it was only full of paper and card. So instead he reached down and pulled the keys free. Then he let himself in.

The flat was well decorated. It was obsessively clean, so Fred took joy in urinating on the bathmat and then in the sink. He had got lucky this time.

A staircase had led him to the top floor flat. He had tried the two below first, but the keys hadn't fit. The flat door opened into a corridor. Right in front was the kitchen, to the left was the living room and to the right was the bedroom with en suite bathroom.

After briefly nosing around, Fred fixed himself a sandwich. He left the bread open so it could mould, and the lid off the butter so the flies could feast too. In the living room he didn't bother removing his soaking rags before he sat down on the suede sofa. He found a pornographic channel on the telly to entertain himself while he finished his sandwich. Drool and food collected on his chin, then he made a mess in his hand from excitement, so he smeared it all on the carpet under his feet. Back in the kitchen he ate bulbs of garlic whole and drank cooking wine from a bottle in the fridge. He checked for any super-strength cider but there was none. Regardless, he had got lucky.

Later he heard voices from below and the creaking of a staircase. Someone was clambering up. It was a man's voice, drunkenly singing to himself, so Fred knew a rape was out of the question. Instead he turned the telly off and slid underneath the king-sized bed. He had to push a rucksack and some dumbbells aside to make room, but in the shadows he was both invisible and at home.

The door to the flat opened and a man walked inside. Footsteps continued into the kitchen, followed by the sound of a microwave humming. After fifteen minutes or so the man came into the bedroom. He sat down on the bed and Fred studied the back of his shoes, only inches away from his fingertips.

Eventually the man undressed and Fred watched naked feet walk in and then out of the bathroom. The mattress sunk, hovering just above his nose, and in the darkness of the room, as the man began to snore, Fred listened to him breathe.

A doorbell rang later in the night. The man rolled out of bed, pulled on a dressing gown and left the flat. He rushed downstairs and let his girlfriend in.

"So, you found your keys?" She asked him.

"Yeah. They were in my bag."

"I left some under the bin for you but now they're gone."

"Forget it. It's cold and I'm tired."

The man held the door for the woman, and they went back upstairs to the flat. Inside, the woman pinched her nose and scowled at him.

"Fucking hell! What is that smell?" She asked, walking quickly around the bed to open a window.

"I can't smell anything," the man smiled and pointed at his blocked nostrils.

Then she undressed and they both got into bed.

"How was your night?" The woman asked but the man was already back asleep. So instead she rolled onto her side before saying: "Love you."

"*Love you too...*" Fred whispered softly from beneath the bed.

The woman murmured.

The next morning Fred watched the man and woman argue. She had woken up early to watch the telly but found it still on the porn channel. She shouted at the man while he was still in bed.

"You are disgusting!"

The man denied it.

"I am ashamed of you! Watching that filth!"

The man got up and got dressed. They argued some more in the kitchen and then the man stormed out of the flat. Fred was cramping-up terribly under the bed and was desperate to crawl free.

The woman started crying and locked herself in the bathroom, so Fred took his opportunity. Standing up and smiling, he placed one ear on the bathroom door and listened to her piss.

When the bath started running he went back and crouched behind the bed again, out of sight. The woman walked out, leaving the bath to fill, and continued into the kitchen. After a few minutes Fred could smell bacon frying.

While the woman cooked, Fred went into the bathroom and took a shit.

He didn't flush.

Instead he did some stretching and decided he couldn't possibly face going under the bed again, so he stood behind the bedroom door. From there he was still hidden and could look through the crack. He watched as the bathroom began to steam up.

When the woman returned to check on her bath, she seemed confused by the turd floating in the toilet, but just shrugged and flushed it away.

While she messed about lighting candles, tuning the bathroom radio and adding lotions to the water, Fred walked into the kitchen and ate one-half of her bacon sandwich. Then he went into the living room and hid inside a cupboard. He couldn't see the reaction of the woman to her missing half sandwich, but there must have been one. The idea amused him.

Over the next hour or so Fred tried to peek under the bathroom door to see the naked woman. He couldn't. And this infuriated him, so instead he went through her draws, playing with her underwear, knickers and bras. When he heard the water starting to drain, he reluctantly decided to go back under the bed again.

He got some thrill from watching the woman's legs as she got dressed in the bedroom. But before he could drag her under and do his worst, the man returned and the pair of them reconciled.

He said he was very drunk when he got home and probably had watched the porn but couldn't remember. He vowed to give up drinking, then she cried, he cried, they hugged, and it was all very beautiful.

Later that day Fred noticed something disturbing, something he hadn't noticed before. There was a cat in the flat. A fat, fluffy little bastard with a crushed-up face and a big tail. It looked spoilt and vile and he hated it immediately. It was a threat.

While the couple watched a film, the cat came into the bedroom and looked at him curiously under the bed. Fred swatted at it, but the cat avoided, instead just watching him in disgust, like every person in the outside world did.

A few hours later when the couple prepared for bed, the little bastard started meowing at him. It was trying to warn them of the danger they were in. It carried on. Meowing and meowing. If it could have pointed at him, it would have.

"What are you meowing at, baby?" The woman asked, as her cat's eyes were locked with those of her unknown intruder.

It meowed again, long and loud, and this time the woman picked it up and put it outside.

Fred had gotten lucky again.

During the night he silently climbed from under the bed and watched the man and woman sleep. He wondered what they were dreaming. He stood there for some time. Maybe hours. Then as sunlight began to claw behind the curtains, he stretched, sighed and returned.

The next day must have been a Monday because both the man and the woman got dressed and left early. The man was trying his hardest to impress the woman, he kept going on and on about how *easy it was* to give up drinking. Then he forced the woman to let him do the breakfast dishes. All the while the cat pranced around the bedroom, humiliating Fred and taunting him.

The woman left first. Then the man finished the dishes and left too.

Fred grinned.

He dragged himself from under the bed and yanked the cat up by the back of its neck. Immediately it went into frenzy, hissing and shaking. He took it into the bathroom and forced its head into the toilet water. He stuffed it down and put his boot on it. He pressed hard, forcing it down and unable to escape. After a minute or so the thrashing stopped and when he took his boot away the toilet was full of white fur and blood. The cat was floating in the pan, twisted and dead.

Fred removed it from the toilet and carried the dripping carcass into the kitchen. He threw it into the sink and refilled it with hot, soapy water.

He had a plan.

And it was coming together perfectly.

During the day Fred got dressed in some of the man's clothes and left the flat. He had found some cash in a draw and used it to buy drugs and alcohol, first from a dealer he knew only a few streets away and then from an off-license on the corner. The owner of the off-license looked at him suspiciously. Fred had stolen booze from there many times before and been chased away by the owner. Now he had turned up in expensive clothes and with a fistful of money.

After his indulgence, Fred went to a Turkish barber a few minutes away. They trimmed his hair and removed his beard with a cut-throat razor.

Back at the flat he got drunk, stuffed himself with food and watched more telly. He drank all the booze he bought and then he finished the cooking wine too. He took all the cans of cider and the bottle and threw them in the recycling bin – right in plain sight.

Pissed and out of his mind, Fred went back under the bed and passed-out.

He awoke to the sound of screaming.

The woman had returned home and found the cat.

Fred smiled.

The screaming turned to crying and soon she was on the phone, telling the man to come home immediately. He did. And when he did, she tore into him:

"You liar! You fucking liar!"

"What? What?" He asked confused.

"You said you'd quit! Look at all this shit!" She howled, pointing at the booze in the recycling bin.

"That's not mine. I swear!"

"Oh fuck off! Whose is it then? Because it's not mine!"

"I... I..."

"You piece of shit! Look what you've done to my cat..."

She dragged him into the kitchen.

"Jesus Christ!" The man shouted. "How did that... I mean... I don't understand!"

"It was you! It was you, you fucker! You left the water in the sink and she drowned! You got pissed and forgot to let the water out! You disgrace! You arsehole!"

The kitchen door slammed shut and shouting continued.

Fred napped for a while, hungover and half-conscious, but all the while smiling to himself as muffled voices, screaming and cursing and crying, carried from the kitchen.

The door to the flat slammed as someone left. Fred crossed his fingers. He hoped it was the man. He hoped he had finally driven him away, so his prey was defenceless. His luck paid off again...

The woman walked into the bedroom – alone. She sat down on the bed and called someone up, a friend or other lover maybe.

"I've left him," she said. "It's done. I can't deal with his bullshit anymore!"

Fred put a hand over his mouth to stop giggling.

"Can you come over? I don't want to be alone."

Then she hung up and just lay on the bed, snoozing and trying to relax, unaware of the obscene amount of peril she was in.

A while later someone knocked on the door and she opened it up. A young man walked in, tan, well-dressed and good looking. The woman started crying and he hugged her. He had a bottle of wine in one hand and with the other he slid it down her back.

She got them glasses and they went into the living room. They chatted and chatted. Fred got out from under the bed and walked down the corridor to listen. She offered to make the mystery man some food and he accepted. They both sounded quite drunk.

As the woman went into the kitchen and the man went for a piss, Fred went into the living room and emptied all the ketamine he had bought into their glasses – more in the man's. Then he clambered into the cupboard and waited. He was good at waiting. Maybe the best in the world. He had proven that.

The man returned and glugged his wine. He was just as hot-and-bothered as Fred was, but the drugs would soon take care of that.

The woman returned and told him it would be a half-hour for the food. While they waited, they began to kiss. Things got exciting very quickly and then, suddenly, they stopped. As the chemicals entered their systems they soon began to fall apart. Fred found it interesting. Soon the man was frozen in place, eyes wide and empty, unable to move or speak. The woman seemed ill, shaking her head and nauseous. It was at this moment that Fred, after days of waiting, took his opportunity.

He exited the cupboard and walked over to the inebriated woman, out of her mind on wine and horse tranquilizers. She looked up at him blearily.

He looked like her partner. Well, now *ex-partner*. Fred had had his hair cut the same way and he was still wearing his clothes.

"Come with me," he said, and she groggily agreed.

They left the other man alone and went into the bedroom.

Fred would have his fun. He deserved it. At least he thought he did.

Then he would change back into his familiar rags and fade back into the alleyways and gutters of the night time. He had had a good thing going. But the streets, and their depravity, were calling his name once again.

"Do I know you?" The woman slurred.

Fred lay her down on the bed and began to undress her.

"You've known me all your life," he replied.

The Chav Who Loved to Ride Horses

"BE GENTLE WHEN YOU PRUNE MY BUSH!" The old woman shouted at me.

Oh go and eat your own shit! I wanted to tell her.

I had been pissed on cider the night before – Hog Death, it was called – nine per cent and tasted like matured urine. It was seeping through my pores and I could taste and smell apple all around me. It was making me gag and this seemed to upset the old woman who was paying me twenty quid to prune her bush. *How did I end up here?* I asked myself, wiping another half-pint of cider from my forehead. Yes, obviously the job centre had sent me. If I hadn't gone I wouldn't have got my money. But *in life* how had I ended up here? Taking shit off some old bitch. Pruning a conifer... a fucking conifer! The most perverted of all bushes. I was supposed to be a famous trap DJ by this point in life. Some compromise...

The old woman finally went inside so I lit a Rothman and sat down.

"I AM NOT PAYING YOU TO SMOKE!" I heard her shout. So I got back up and started snipping at the bush again.

The sun was vile, trying to break me but I wouldn't give in. No way! Twenty quid and a free afternoon awaited. I knew my mates were already nostril deep in a few grams of cheap speed. They would be bugging me to join them soon enough.

After an hour or so the bush took shape and the old tit seemed to take a bit kinder to me. She made me a cup of tea, but in the grips of her dementia had put two spoonfuls of salt, not sugar, into it.

She held eye contact with me as I took the first sip. I felt obliged to swallow.

"Lovely!" I lied, trying to hold down the Hog Death and ignore the taste of warm brine around my teeth.

"Well then, continue drinking!" she demanded.

Jesus Christ! Was she going to watch me drink the whole thing?

I sipped again and felt my stomach rumble. Maybe she knew it was salt. Maybe she had done it on purpose.

I drank the entire tea and felt like fainting. She smiled and took the cup back. "Another?"

"No thank you ma'am."

I gargled, coughed, nearly choked and then phlegmed a nice gloop onto her grass. This was a mistake, because my body then decided to *get rid of everything else*. I rushed past the conifer and over to a fence line.

Bracing myself against the posts, I bent at the waist and watered the flowers with some Hog Death. I felt truly pathetic. The sun continued to scorch my back and the vomit below me bubbled. But then something tapped me on the neck.

Straightening up quickly I saw it was a horse. He was leaning over the fence and looking at me with intrigue.

"Alright mate, how are you doing?" I asked.

I'd never seen a horse before.

I'd seen them on the pub telly when the National was on, but never in person. I was born inner-city. Raised inner-city. Stayed inner-city. No greenery. Just concrete. I think I even had concrete in my blood. Jesus, I didn't see grass until I was sixteen on a school trip! Until then I thought grass was what you bought off the Jamaican kids for a tenner a bag.

The horse neighed at me and rubbed his powerful head against my trembling hand. He was enormous and his coat was the colour of old silver jewellery. As he pulled away his giant nostrils inhaled and seemed to drag some of my hangover with them.

"My name's Jez, what's your name?" I asked and patted him again.

He seemed to like me, which made a difference from every other snob who lived nearby. They hated me. They hated my pasty skin, my cheap cigarettes, my shaven head, my Cabrini tracksuit, my Makita radio, my speedgarage, my Nissan Micra and my blow off valve.

But not this fella. This big, beautiful beast didn't think I was *scum* or *common*. For the first time since this morning; since the postman had given me the eye, since the old woman had started moaning, since the young toffs had walked passed me laughing and whispering to each other... since the beginning of this hellish day, I had finally found a friend.

"EXCUSE ME!" I heard a familiar voice shriek.

I sighed and gave my new friend a final pat on the nose.

"Sorry," I shrugged. "He's a lovely horse, isn't he?"

"Yes I know that," the old woman said and began pointing towards the conifer.

I plodded back over to it. "What's his name, if you don't mind me asking?"

"Enoch."

The conifer took longer than expected, partly because of the weather, partly because of my MacGowan-esque condition and partly because of my preoccupation with Enoch the horse. I kept looking over to see him watching me with equal interest. As I tidied up the clippings, I decided we were kindred spirits.

When I finished work the fantasies about speed and lager were stronger than ever, but the old woman wasn't done:

"Young man!" She shrieked as I started up the Micra.

"Yes?"

"Do you want some more work tomorrow?"

My soul screamed *no* but my wallet screamed *yes*. "I suppose so."

"You *suppose* or you *do?*"

"I will. Yes. Thank you."

"There are some more conifers over there..." She pointed but I didn't bother to look.

I told her I would be back the next morning and then I set off home. The drive was long and boring. Just queues upon queues upon queues. No horns. No road rage. Just dreary humming of engines, bad radio reception and a strange lingering image of that horse in my brain.

Coked to the gills I prowled the living room floor, recounting tales of Enoch to my delinquent friends that twitched and gurned on the old settee. Music was on, it might have been blaring but I didn't realise. I was too focused on describing the horse to them:

"Man, you should have seen it! At least twenty foot high! A head like a... like a..."

"Horse?" Someone whispered.

I noticed Terry wasn't paying attention and this annoyed me.

"What's wrong with you, Terry?"

"Ahhk! Me skin!" He moaned, rubbing invisible blotches up and down his arms.

"What's wrong with it?" I asked.

"It's tender. I just ate beef."

Terry had a bovine-intolerance meaning he couldn't eat brisket or loin. I ignored him and tried to carry on, but evidentially my friends had had enough of me:

"All right, McCririck, will you give us a fucking rest?"

"Yeah! Shut up!"

"Ha ha! Horse spaz!"

I swatted the air. *What fools!* I thought. They were more bothered about Poundland and who-shagged-who and what imported team of athletes had done best on the television.

I walked out onto the balcony and looked down into Edward Gein. We were up high. Beyond the heavens even. With so much ampage thundering through my system, the plummet down seemed more like a dare than an act of insanity. But when I looked into the vacant skies I could only see Enoch's dark eyes. *What is it about this horse?* I asked myself. Then I realised I was asking the wrong person.

"Give me my share," I said to Terry when I walked back into the room.

"Are you off, Jez?" Someone asked.

"Yes-I-am. I'm going to see Enoch!"

I grabbed my share of the speed and went for the door.

I parked the Micra within the darkness of the country lane and then I walked onto the farm. Through the purple night I could see the silhouette of the old woman's house. The lights were off and she was probably deep in slumber, dreaming of conifers and table salt. But she wasn't on my mind. Although smothering her with some tartan cushion did seemed appealing, it was Enoch that I wanted to see.

In the darkness of the field I could hear hoofs tearing back-and-forth into soft ground. There was neighing somewhere in the shadows and my chest filled with excitement. I felt like a child on Christmas, like an alki at opening time.

"Hello, my mate!" I said, clambering the fence and perching on top of it.

A huge mass of black came towards me and held steady. It was Enoch, he was studying me, registering whether I was friend or foe. Eventually his grey colour cut through the dark.

I felt close to the animal. I felt like we were brothers, separated at birth, one raised a chav and the other raised a horse.

"It's me – Jez," I said and he seemed to take comfort in that. Then he neighed and turned, showing me his arse. Was this some kind of insult or compliment? I asked myself as he started stamping at the ground.

Suddenly something took me over. Something crazy but something so right.

I let go of the fence –

I jumped –

I landed on his back –

And in a bolt we exploded into the night.

I felt like something that didn't exist, flying at speeds impossible, through a galaxy that hadn't been born yet. All around me was thick, unending black, yet I could feel wind and space hurtle past my face. The power of the beast below me was frightening at first but eventually it was more thrilling than any street speed could be.

Enoch grinded to a halt and I fell into the back of his neck.

But then something happened to shatter our little moment:

A light burnt across the field.

I turned quickly. It was coming from the old woman's house. She must have heard the commotion outside and turned her bedroom light on.

"Shit!" I managed to gurn to myself, still twisted on amphetamines while straddling a stranger's horse.

As if understanding me, Enoch began back towards the fence, aiding in my escape. I jumped the post and landed on the grass just as I heard a door creak open. Quickly I darted into the shadows of the conifers. "*I'll be back, old buddy!*" I whispered, just as the old woman started shouting.

That night I went home and started mixing a new track.

It was classic trap. Old-school batty man trap.

And I called it *Enoch*.

The next day the old woman was suspicious of my involvement in last night's antics. She looked at me cross-eyed, more so, and didn't offer me any tea-with-salt. I ignored. I was coming down from the speed (which was hell) but I had a bottle of Hog Death in my bag and was eagerly awaiting a chance to have it.

Enoch was prowling the fields, restless and eager to get at me again. Soon! Soon, my friend! I thought to myself as I hacked mindlessly away at the conifers.

"Go and fetch me some petrol!" She shouted at me at one point. It wasn't in my job description but I went and did it anyway at a station just around the corner. When I came back she was in the field. She had a harness around Enoch's head and was holding him steady. In the other hand she had a piece of bamboo and every few seconds lashed him across the nose with it. He pulled his head and shrieked after every strike. But with some kind of twisted strength the old woman held onto him.

I dropped the petrol and hopped the fence, snatching the stick out of her hand.

"How dare you! Give me that back!" She demanded, letting go of the reigns and letting Enoch bolt.

"What the fuck are you doing?" I asked her, feeling my hand tremble, ready to lash her across the face.

"You need to discipline an animal!" she said. "The same could be said for you!" And she pulled the stick away from me. Then, only with the flick of her wrist, she slapped me on the chest with it. "Now get back to work or I will call the police!"

I turned away and started walking back to the bushes.

"And if you don't do a good job..." I could hear her continuing behind me. "...I will do much worse!"

I paid her no attention. Enoch was over at the far end of the field, throwing his head to-and-fro, probably nursing his wounds. Meanwhile, inside me something was burning dangerously.

"I'm going to the post office. Be done by the time I am back!" The old woman shouted at me. I could hear her Honda Jazz starting up and driving away.

As the sound of her engine faded, I undid the canister of petrol. I doused the conifers and set them alight, smiling all the while. Then I hopped the fence and walked over to him.

I felt like a father ready to console a weeping child. "Here, here..." I said softly and patted him on the side. He knew I was no enemy and let me stand close and reassure him. "We need to get out of here Enoch... I need to get away from the scum and the drugs. And you... you need to get away from that old hag!" As if understanding me, he nodded his head and I jumped aboard once again.

"FREEDOM, ENOCH! FREEEEEEDOM!"

We tore across the field and sailed over the fence posts. Onto the front garden Enoch seemed to know where he was going. He went through the front gates and turned left onto the narrow country lane. We continued down quickly. I was exhilarated. I was feeling more *right* than any other time in my life! As we reached the end of the road I saw a familiar Honda Jazz turn the corner. The door opened and the old woman got out. She started waving her fist and shouting something as we galloped towards her.

"FREEEEEEEDOM!" I shouted as we trampled the old bastard underfoot.

Boy, I couldn't wait to show the lads at Ed Gein my new horse.

The Christopher Hagen Jamboree

I first noticed the window when I was walking home from The Prince. It was on the second floor of an old Victorian house. I assumed, as with most of them on the road, the house had been converted into flats. It was the top floor window, and behind red drapes I saw the stationary figures of men and women, hands cocked for cigarette-holding and the pulsing of an orange glow behind them. The feint sound of music, old time jazz, reverberated through the window and the hum of sophisticated conversation joined it. I watched in awe.

That was where I wanted to be. I wanted to be a part of that circle. I went to the pubs almost daily, The Prince, The Horse, and all the cheaper dives in between. I had a wide friendship group, but it was superiority that I yearned for. I could talk shit with anyone. But who would talk Brahms and Heidegger with me?

I paused under the streetlamp and watched the figures. They were still. As I watched them I tried to make out the conversation that drifted down. It was past midnight and I was past drunk, so I staggered across the road and walked up to the house. By the oak door were three different bells, all labelled. Flat three was labelled as *Christopher Hagen*.

"What a name!" I slurred to myself and pressed it.

From above I heard a bell ringing.

I waited.

Nothing.

So I rang again.

After another failed ring I lit a cigarette and crossed back over the road. A group of drunken girls were walking up, so I pretended to tie my shoelace until they passed. I didn't want them to see me perversely staring at the window. But when they left, and their inebriated howls faded, I turned my attention back...

The scene hadn't changed. The drapes quivered slightly, but the figures remained where they were, the music and talking continued, and I remained insignificant and unnoticed.

I sighed. I was doomed to a mediocre life.

So I walked home.

The next afternoon I was in the pub again. I was talking with a couple of friends about the strange window.

"I've seen it before," Martin said. "When I drive home from working nights. It's the only window with a light on that late, facing the Alcester road. You can see it all the way up the hill. It's pretty strange."

"Strange?" I jolted, for some reason feeling offended. "I'd love to go in! Imagine what it's like inside!"

"Why don't you then?" Alex butted in. "Ask to go up."

"No, no..." I shook my head. "That would be weird."

"No mate," Alex continued, belching Carling at me before carrying on. "*Weird* is watching it during the night, by yourself, from the street. That's fucking weird."

"Yeah! Ha-ha!" Martin agreed.

They mocked me. The mongols mocked me.

So I laughed it off and stood up to get a round, silently vowing to myself to return to the house again.

After drinking with Martin and Alex for a few more hours they said it was time to leave. They both had shifts on the buses. So instead I sat at the bar. The barmaid was new and wasn't making conversation, so I stared at the coloured bottles of liquor on the shelf and wondered, too much, about the window and the flat.

"Young man," someone said, and I ignored. I assumed it wasn't aimed at me. But then I felt something prod me in the arm.

An old, rotting man was stood beside me. He had an empty glass of stout and was waiting to be served.

"No, I'm not waiting, mate. Go ahead," I said. But he prodded me again. "What?"

"I overheard you talking about the window, the window with the light on."

My interest ignited. "Yes?"

"Stay away from it!" He waved a finger in my face and then flagged the barmaid down.

"But why?" I asked, taking him by the arm (and thus making a mental note to bleach my hand later).

"Just stay away!" He growled. "I know *people like you* are interested. But *people like you* don't come back."

What did he mean by that? I asked myself as he waddled back to a seat in the corner. He sipped the radiator water (allegedly stout) and eyed me strangely. Although he had warned me against returning, what he had instead done had made me even more obsessed. I now had a plan, and it was simple:

Get pissed.

Ignore advice.

Those two rules had got me far in life, so I would not betray them.

Walking up the Alcester road I was half expecting the lights to be off inside the flat. But before I even reached it, the soft sound of jazz and whispers carried down the street. I smiled to myself as I saw the building. The lights were on behind the red drapes, figures stood in similar position, and the feeling inside me was the same – desperation. Desperation to get inside and prove myself worthy. No longer would I need Alex or Martin or other drunken arseholes in my life. I could meet real people.

Again I crossed the road and again I pressed the bell for Christopher Hagen.

There was no response. And as I glanced at the door, imagining the staircase behind, I noticed a new sign had been hung on it. My eyes slowly adjusted, then I read:

Flat three party by invite only.

Please leave name and address below.

Note: not all applicants will be accepted.

With a shaking, sweating hand I scribbled my name and address onto the paper from a fountain pen that was dangling beside it from a piece of twine. I ended it with *please please please please please*. Did he know? Did Christopher Hagen know just how much I needed this? I had to make him aware.

And then I rushed home, with some delusional part of my brain hoping an invite would already be waiting for me...

The next two days were torturous. I took them off work, just waiting by the door, clutching a can of something alcoholic and waiting for the postman. As he walked up the drive I would open, wearing only my boxers, hair unkempt and crust around my eyes. "HURRY UP! HURRY UP!" I would shout. And he would throw bills and chicken-shop vouchers at me, then run away. But no invite.

On day three I lay-in, hungover and depressed. He had obviously rejected my request for an invite.

"You made a fool of yourself!" I shouted. "All that *please-pleasing*. He probably thought you were quoting The Beatles!"

I needed air. I needed to forget the flat. The window. The light. The people. The possibilities.

But as I stormed out of my home, I saw a single peach-coloured envelope lying on the door mat. The postman had not delivered it. Someone else had.

I tore it open and read the words inside. Beautiful calligraphy writing told me, in Olde English, that I had been invited to an evening party at the Hagen residence. My life felt suddenly complete.

I called up Martin and Alex and told them, and they told me to *fuck off*. I went out into Kings Heath and bought a suit from a charity shop that someone had probably died of shingles in. Then I pampered myself with cologne and Brylcreem and stole a bottle of knock-off brandy from a Bargain Booze. By the evening time I was half brain-damaged from the amount of aftershave I had inhaled. But I was ready. I was ready to meet my destiny.

As I stumbled down the Alcester road clutching the brandy, I knew certainly that my life would be different from now on. I thought momentarily about the old man who warned me away. What did he know! I smiled to myself.

Night descended as I waited outside Christopher Hagen's flat. I waited eagerly across the road. The window was dark and seemed almost lifeless. But I knew better. I knew the potential from inside.

The invite said arrive at nine o' clock but I was waiting from seven. I took several hits from the brandy and knew that Chris wouldn't mind. I thought of myself like a beat poet, beat poets drank booze to the extreme *and they* were considered gods.

Suddenly the light switched on from the flat. Figures were already stood in position. Then a moment later, as if coming from nothing, jazz and conversation both began in sync. I thought it was strange. I hadn't seen anyone go into the flat in the two hours I had been stood there. But my worries were soon forgotten, I was striding across the street and up to the front door.

I pressed the bell and almost immediately (as if someone had been watching me cross the road) a voice whispered softly down the intercom:

"Come on up..."

I smiled and heard the door be electronically unlocked.

I pushed it open and headed in. The downstairs was dark and dingy. The walls were full of damp but that didn't bother me. Downstairs wasn't upstairs. I would be going upstairs. Up to Christopher Hagen's flat! As I charged up something was rumbling in my stomach, but I ignored it.

At the top of the stairs I saw another door. It was painted black and had beautiful stained glass obscuring the light from within. Someone moved from behind it and I heard a lock be undone. I smiled. I was almost there.

I knocked but no one answered. The sound of Chet Baker and upper-class discussions were probably too loud for anyone to hear me, so I turned the handle myself and stepped inside.

The flat was art deco. It reminded me of a scene from The Great Gatsby, very nineteen-twenties. Lots of blacks and whites and golds. But... there was nobody around.

"Hello?" I called out into the open space.

Conversation and music were coming from a room ahead. I stepped forward, pacing across the unblemished landing up to a second door. Then I turned the handle and stepped inside. At first I felt relieved – I had found the party! People were all around, dressed in suits, holding champagne glasses, some even had cigarette holders. Lots of people to talk to, to laugh with, to get drunk with, to befriend. But almost immediately I realised that would be impossible:

They were all mannequins.

Every single one of them was a wax figure, dressed up and positioned as if attending a New Year's ball from the roaring twenties.

In disbelief I began walking between them, the rows and rows of men and women mannequins all in different scenarios, some kissing, some dancing, others in conversation, others pouring drinks or sharing cigarettes. I stared into their shiny faces. They were all smiling. But their eyes were glassy and dead.

In the corner of the living room I noticed an old-style phonograph speaker with a horn. The sound of jazz and conversation was coming from it, loudly. Was this some kind of joke? I put the brandy down on a nearby table and felt immediately uneasy. Where was Christopher Hagen? Did he exist? Someone had spoken to me down the intercom and someone had also unlocked the flat door for me.

"I don't like this," I said out loud to the nearest mannequin. But he ignored me.

I quickly ran back to the front door. I pulled at the handle but it had been locked again, most probably while I was distracted in the living room. Now I was trapped. A fly in a cobweb. A dumb idiot who had ignored the warnings of an old man the day before.

For some reason I went back in. The mannequins hadn't changed and the music and conversation were still blaring. I went across to the window to try and attract someone's attention from below. As I pulled back the drapes I saw someone across the street outside. It was a young man, drunk and dishevelled. He was looking up at me in awe, as if *he too* wanted to be up here. Another fool!

As I looked down and prepared to signal for help, I saw something in the window's reflection move in the room behind me.

It was one of the mannequins.

Prophet of the Substation Wall

The council sent me to clean some graffiti. It was written on the brick wall of an electrical substation. Inside these substations electrical power from the grid was dropped, so it could be used domestically. The problem was what it said. All over the brick wall facing the street, the pedestrians and the traffic, were the words:

SUSAN BILL SUCKS MONKEY ELEPHANT DICKS

Susan Bill was the local councillor and a woman I had met once before. To be honest it did make me laugh, the first time I saw it. The woman was vile. Only last year she was caught using moneys allocated for poor-side's youth club to take a holiday in Devon. Embezzlement and fraud I could understand, but holidaying in Devon? What kind of shit would do that? ...well, maybe the kind of shit that sucks monkey elephant dicks (whatever that means).

I got to work with some brick acid and took my time. I mixed it half-and-half with water and scrubbed the letters until they faded.

Years ago in my teens I would have considered myself a traitor for what I was doing. I was part of the anarchist circle, I was trying to bring about the revolution. But anger calms with age, every storm settles, and those whose storm's don't settle either live their shortened lives in depression or loneliness. You can't be angry forever. Sooner or later you realise the system was designed to withstand revolt.

"You will make a lot of people happy by cleaning that," a middle-aged man told me as I was finishing up.

"Is that so?" I asked as I lit a cigarette.

"Yes. Mrs Bill has done some truly brilliant things for the local area and the church. It is absolutely outrageous that some young piffler should graffitise such nonsense."

Graffitise wasn't a word. But I couldn't be bothered to correct him.

I also couldn't be bothered to correct the *truly brilliant things* that Susan Bill had done.

Well... she was very supportive, financially and otherwise, of a local group of nonces called *the parish*. She presented prizes at their summer fetes, raised money for their church roof and so on. Yet obviously the youth clubs of poor-side weren't in Susan Bill's big picture. No, those kids went without while the church went with. I looked away from the old man as an inner John Lydon began to flare up for the first time in a while.

"Good day," he said.

"Yes."

I tidied my things away and went home.

I went straight home. Not to the pub and not to the bookies.

I had to be careful with myself.

Next morning was Saturday – the Jewish day of rest. I wasn't Jewish but I did enjoy potato pancakes and hibernating on a Saturday. So I woke up late, cooked some pancakes naked in the kitchen, ate them in the living room and watched an episode of *Star Trek*. It was at this moment I realised, as I sometimes did, that maybe my friends whose storms never settled had ended up better than me. At least they had died with their morals intact and not lived on as a sell-out.

Anyway, it wasn't until I turned my phone on that I realised work had been calling me all morning. I usually had Saturdays off, so I called them back to find out what was going on.

"Hello?" I asked, when Big gay Tim answered.

"Is there a reason why the graffiti wasn't cleaned?" Big gay Tim asked.

"I cleaned the graffiti."

"I've just been past it. It's still there."

"Big g-, I mean Tim, I cleaned it off! I was there all day!"

He sighed. I could hear him chewing something on the other end of the phone, either a young boy's ass or one of those toffee pastries he loved. "Just get it done," he said and hung up on me.

FUCK! I was pissed off. I showered as quickly as I could and brushed my teeth, then I got changed and walked down to the van in the estate's car park.

During the night some tramp had tried to open the van door to get to the tools. I could tell from the bloodstains. Previously, tired of thievery, I had superglued carpet grips to the underside of the handles, so when someone unsuspectingly tried it, they pulled the grips into their fingers.

I was glad in a way that I had foiled the robbery, but the blood on the door only added to my frustration.

After cleaning the AIDs off the door, I drove across town. Usually I took it easy when I drove, I was on the council's time, but today was different, I was on *my* time.

When I arrived at the substation I glanced out the window and saw something that confused the fuck out of me.

The graffiti was back.

"Oh fuck off," I growled to myself, sliding out of the van and wandering over.

    SUSAN BILL STILL SUCKS MONKEY ELEPHANT DICKS

    AND SO DO YOU! COUNCIL CLEANING SLAVE!

"Fucking bastard!" I turned and went straight to the van. I mixed the acid half-and-half again and scrubbed at the words. This time I worked with anger and got it done in half the time. I realised this anger had little to do with my wasted Saturday (...I wasted every Saturday anyway!) it was to do with the reality check that this vandal was giving me. He was poking fun at a part of my life that I disgusted.

When the cleaning was done, I was pouring with sweat and panting. So I called up big gay Tim, who was also probably sweating and panting, but in his case in a public lavatory.

"Uh-huh?" He asked, over the sound of a pastry being devoured.

"Done," I coughed.

"I should hope so," and then he hung up.

I grabbed the phone and put it between my teeth, trying to bite it in half.

Get a hold of yourself! Some voice of reason said. But I was getting close to the edge.

"Man, oh man! You're pushing me, baby!" I waved my fist at some invisible enemy and then got back into the van.

The pub was calling.

I hadn't been to The Fox in over a fortnight. I didn't drink nearly as much as I had in my youth but recently (well, two weeks) I had cut down big time. I didn't drink in the flat anymore. I didn't drink alone and I didn't drink during the weeks. In fact that slush of Carling that ran down my throat was the first alcohol in my system for fourteen days… and fuck me, had it been missed!

"Can you believe it?" I explained my story to the owner, whose name I couldn't remember.

"Well, he sure is putting in the effort."

"I know, little bastard!"

"He's not wrong."

"About what?"

"Susan Bill is a fucking arsehole."

"He didn't say she fucks arseholes, he said she sucks monkey elephant dicks."

"Same thing."

"And he said I did too!"

He shrugged and smirked, so I told him to *do one*.

I drank in peace for a while and wondered about the rakehell who had taken it upon themselves to wage war against Susan Bill. It was only a small town, divided down the middle - rich and poor, but I supposed this kind of thing could happen anywhere. Injustice was indiscriminate. In a way I admired them. Years ago it could have been me doing this, and looking back on it I would have been proud.

Just coming up to closing time, I'd had my share. I dropped a few empty pint glasses onto the bar and nodded at the nameless owner. He nodded back. As I staggered towards the door a couple of young lads came in, shrieking with laughter as they did.

"Have you lot seen the graffiti on the box down the road?" They hollered to anyone who would listen.

I paused – mid wobble.

"What graffiti?" I slurred at them.

They told me where. But I already had a suspicion...

It was back.

HOW MUCH DOES SUSAN BILL PAY YOU, MONKEY MAN?

It wasn't about Susan Bill anymore. The vandal was targeting me! I was too drunk to do anything. Instead I just stood in disbelief, reading the line over and over again, furiously intrigued. I didn't get paid enough for this – to take this kind of abuse, to work seven days a week.

Eventually I decided to walk home.

I'd be working Sunday now as well.

The next morning, hungover or not, I got up early and drove down to the substation. Big, gay Tim hadn't called me yet so maybe he hadn't seen it. I mixed the acid seventy-thirty and used thicker gauntlets to protect my hands. Then I got to work. *How much does Susan Bill pay you monkey man?* I had to stare at those words, I had to let that insult burn into my vision and my mind for two hours as I scrubbed and scrubbed, sweated and sweated, burnt and burnt as the acid ran down the gloves and onto my arms.

Minimum wage would be his answer. Peanuts. Fuck all. But I tried not to focus on that.

When the graffiti was gone, I hoped for a peaceful day. After packing up and going home I watched some porn, ran a bath, ate a sandwich in the bath, emptied the bath and fell asleep on the couch.

Monday morning rolled around. So I brushed my teeth, lit a cigarette and drove to the office.

The traffic was dead and I was feeling in a better mood. I could finally get on with some different work. I knew the grass needed cutting at several spots around town. And I hadn't done roadkill duty for a few days, so surely there was a fair bit of death to clean off the country lanes. But, when I got to the office and saw big gay Tim at the coffee machine, he told me plain and simple:

"Graffiti duty."

"WHAT? Where now? I was doing that substation all weekend! Can't you give me a break from graffiti? I'll do it tomorrow or Wednesday, wherever it is. The grass needs cutting and the –,"

"Back at the substation," he said and threw a piece of pastry into his mouth.

"Wait, what?"

"Yes. It's back again," he smiled at me, with crumbs and toffee all over his ass-hungry lips.

I was in disbelief. Back again? This was becoming a fucking joke.

I got straight into the van and drove. No matter how much I wanted that big, gay bastard to be wrong, when I arrived at the substation I saw that he wasn't. It was there again:

JOIN ME, FELLOW PROLETARIAT!

SUSAN BILL SUCKS MONKEY ELEPHANT DICKS!

The classic slogan was now triple in size to the original. In my time of cleaning and battling this vandal I had somehow made the situation worse.

Join him?

Why the fuck would I join him? He was a loser. A man who painted slurs onto public property for a living.

"Listen to yourself..." I started grumbling as I pulled brushes and acid out of the van. *"He's a loser because he paints slurs onto public property? Well you're the loser who cleans them off! You're even worse!"*

I shook my head angrily and stormed over to the substation, but I paused. Somehow I couldn't. Not yet. I just couldn't muster up the energy or the be-arsed-ness to start cleaning it again. Instead I sat down on the tub of acid, lit a cigarette and stared at the words in front of me.

Join him?

How could I do that? By refusing to clean it off? They'd just get someone else to do it.

The vandal was clearly unhinged, so I briefly looked around to see if anyone was watching me (maybe he hung around and admired his work?) but all I saw was a snobby looking man in a BMW, parked up nearby and talking loudly on the phone. I ignored him and finished the cigarette. Then I heard a car door slam behind me. The BMW man was out and walking over.

"I can see why this isn't getting cleaned off!" He said.

My fists were already balled up. "Excuse me?"

"How do you expect to clean that rubbish off if you're just sat on your behind?"

"Who the fuck are you?"

His face lit up. "I AM SUSAN BILL'S HUSBAND! I AM SEBASTIAN BILL! YOU WILL NOT DISRESPECT ME!"

Jesus Christ, god-complex or what? I thought as I threw my cigarette away. "Sorry, sir."

"Do you like your job?" He asked, trembling with rage.

Fuck no. "Yes, sir."

"Do you want to keep your job?"

I'd like to stick my job up your wife's – "Yes, sir."

"Then I recommend you wise up!" He started wagging his finger in my face. "Clean it off! Keep it cleaned off! Mrs Bill is not happy at all!"

"Will do, sir. Right away, sir."

God I hated myself.

I hated myself more than Susan Bill, more than her husband, more than big gay Tim who ate pastries and treated me like shit, and more than this vandal who had turned my life into a living hell. You know why? Out of all of them, I was the only phony. The only man who betrayed his morals. They were greedy, horrible bastards and they knew they were, they lived that way and stayed that way. I had never been like this. A boot-licker. A *yes sir, no sir* commoner who took shit off the rich man and took it with a smile. Nevertheless, I picked up my brush and started scrubbing again.

When I finished I was exhausted – physically, emotionally, in every possible way. But I had an idea. In the glove box of the van was a permanent marker. I brought it back over to the substation and started scribbling on the bricks. I kept the writing small, so you would never notice it unless you were up close. I left him a message:

Listen mate, I appreciate what you're doing. I'm not your enemy. But this graffiti is fucking my life up! They'll give me the sack if you don't stop!

I smiled to myself. No one had seen. Maybe the vandal would take pity on me, a fellow proletariat, and stop his activities. Then I'd just pop back and scrub my little message off.

I got back into the van and drove to The Fox. I decided to wait their until later and then check back on the results. After a couple of pints I became unusually hot-and-bothered. It had been months since I'd had a woman, but The Fox was hardly the place to find one.

The only woman in there looked like a mass murderer. She was about twenty stone, and would have to be scientifically proven as female to me. She had the most enormous pair of deformed breasts I'd ever seen. The cleavage wasn't satisfying. It looked like a Turkish man's ass with all the hair, tan and fat. It scared me. Killed my libido. So I left.

My heart sank when I arrived back at the substation. There was graffiti back up again. Jesus Christ! Fuck! Did this man not sleep? Did he just live solely to deface the electrical substation?

Obviously the monkey elephant dick stuff was up again, but there was also a smaller message for me. I was eager (but disappointed) to see what it said:

Susan Bill stole two grand from the poor-side youth club to go holidaying with her husband.

That money was going to take the kids to the beach for a day.

Shame on her! And shame on you for working for her!

Something sunk in my stomach, like an anchor with its chains around my heart. The woman was a cunt. And I was working for her. Not just an arrogant, ignorant, self-centred cunt. But a cunt who stole money off poor kids. The vandal was right. I should be ashamed. Where had I gone wrong? It was scary. I had sold my soul, and if that wasn't bad enough, I hadn't even noticed it was gone.

I didn't know what to do. I smoked a cigarette. Read it all again. And went home. In my dreams an idea came to me. It wasn't a good idea. But it was the only one I had.

"You're on thin ice," a soft voice whispered into my ear the next morning at work.

Big gay Tim was smirking behind me.

"What do you mean?" I asked.

"The graffiti problem hasn't been resolved. You've failed."

"Oh just listen here Tim, I –,"

He raised a hand for me to *shut up* and then beckoned me towards his office. I had to walk down a long corridor, staring at the back of his fat arse. He was carrying a box of pastries and I could hear them knocking about inside. This was worse than hell.

When we reached his office, he held the door. It wasn't out of courteousness. He just didn't want to go in first. And when I stepped inside, I realised why…

There she was.

The woman who sucked monkey elephant dicks.

"Here he is, Mrs Bill," Big gay Tim said to her.

She was vile looking.

Short bobbed hair with dyed tips looked like bloody daggers. Her skin was red and dry, like some kind of vaginal-eczema had spread to her face. Her eyes were bright blue but with a thick glaze, thicker than the glaze on big gay Tim's pastry crust.

"I'd like an explanation," she said.

"I don't really have one, ma'am."

"And why not?" She hissed.

"I'm not sure how it's my responsibility, ma'am. I can only clean the graffiti off once it's there. I'm not a policeman. I can't mind the wall twenty-four-seven."

"And why not?"

Was she being serious? I looked at big gay Tim for some help, but he was proving about as useful as tits on a boy. I was on my own. "If you cannot control this problem then I will have to find someone who can," she said, shaking her head and finally looking away from me.

"I'm so sorry about this, Mrs Bill," Big gay Tim spoke.

"You can just shut up!" She shouted. I tried not to laugh. "Do you know how embarrassing this has been for me and my family?" Tim sunk down in his chair. "Some idiot out there! Common-as-muck, no doubt! Vandalising public property! Writing slanderous things about me! And what have you done? WHAT HAVE YOU DONE?"

He said nothing.

"I want this, this…" she pointed at me. "Useless man gone by the end of the week!"

"Yes, Mrs Bill."

"And I want the graffiti sorted. ONCE AND FOR ALL!"

"Yes, Mrs Bill. All I can do is offer my sincerest –,"

But before he could finish, she was up and out of the office. The door was slamming back into the frame before either of us had a chance to think.

There was a moment of awkward silence.

"Thanks for all the support there, Tim," I said and stuck my thumb up at him.

"You did this to yourself," he said, trying to save face after the whupping he just received.

"Did I? Did I really?"

"Yes," he stuffed some more pastry into his mouth and sucked at his fingers. "Now you heard Mrs Bill… out by the end of the week!"

I turned on my heels and walked out of the office. I closed the door behind me but could still hear him eating. It was nauseating. And I was manic. It was just at that moment that Brenda, the council treasurer, passed me by.

"Are you okay?" she asked.

"Sure am," I smiled. "Tim wants me to change the lock on the safe. Care to take me to it?"

"Follow me."

"Thanks Brenda."

"I hope it's a nice secure lock," she started blabbering on. "The safe is all full after the church fete. They're raising money for a new roof."

"Oh are they? How very lovely."

I followed after her.

I was sat in The Fox, absolutely smashed. I'd ordered the entire pub a pint and was helping myself to an eighth. The owner, who I'd established as Al, was talking to me while I propped up the bar.

"Nice settlement," he said, shaking his head.

"It's the least they could do, all the blood, sweat and tears I put into that bollocks."

"Still, I don't get it. First thing they're telling us they have no money, next thing they're paying out their staff like that!"

"Don't think too hard about it," I nodded.

"Very well. So what're you going to do with it then?"

"Holiday, I reckon. Get away from here."

"Oh yeah?"

"Yeah."

I left The Fox around midnight and staggered around town. I had a few grand in my pocket and would finally be able to leave. But something wasn't quite right. I had finished my job and stolen the council's money. In a way I hoped that would restore some pride in myself – but it didn't. I still felt like shit and a sell-out. I still didn't feel like the real *me*. Like I used to.

I found myself back at the substation. The graffiti from the other day was still there, and the vandal's response to my plea for sympathy. Oh, how pathetic I had been! I re-read the correspondence and felt sick. Then guilty. Then, finally, I knew what I had to do.

Returning home, I opened up the van, I was still steaming drunk, but I managed to drive back to the substation.

In the back of the van I found my tub of brickwork tools. I grabbed out a hammer and bolster, then I knocked out some mortar in a joint between two bricks on the substation wall. I did it just below the vandal's response to my message.

Then I took the wad of cash I stole from the church fete and rolled it into a tight tube. Carefully I slid it into the gap and wrote a final word beneath it:

Sorry. With an arrow pointing at the money. Maybe the kids would go to the beach after all.

The next morning my phone was ringing and so was my head. It was big gay Tim. I rejected the call and quickly fried up some bacon. By now I guessed he had realised what I'd done. He might have called the police. Only I guessed he would be too embarrassed. He wouldn't want Susan Bill finding out. Instead he'd try to scare me into giving it back.

Too late now, fatso! I wish I could have told him.

"What to do now?" I asked myself as the bacon sizzled below. I had slept in. It was midday. I was out of work. Skint. And soon headed for prison. But did I care? Did I fuck. And that new found apathy restored some faith in myself. I decided to hand myself in later. But before that, I wanted to check that the vandal had got his money.

Was I being naïve? Who knows...

Maybe he was just a crack head with too much time on his hands?

Maybe he'd just spend the money on hookers or crack, or a hooker's crack?

I didn't care. Even if some total tramp bought a prostitute, that still seemed more noble than a church being reroofed.

Strolling down the street without a care in the world I was happy, right up until I saw what had happened:

There was fencing all around the substation and a digger was parked nearby. They had knocked it down. Under orders from Susan Bill, the power had been re-directed, and the old brick substation had been torn to the ground. My mouth was dry. I rushed up to the fencing and pulled myself over. I could hear builders shouting from by the digger, but I ignored them.

It wasn't the money. Fuck the money!

I wanted him to know. I wanted him to know that I wasn't like the rest of them! I wanted him to know I cared about those kids. I cared about sticking it to those council bastards!

It was just rubble. A huge heap of bricks, broken roof tiles and mangled timber. It was lost. The money. The graffiti. My pride. I started clawing at the bricks in desperation, cutting my fingers, all the while the shouting grew and grew.

"CALL THE POLICE!" Someone shouted.

And then I saw it.

One piece of the wall still clung together. The mortar had held several bricks strong and the bricks had been brave against the wrecking power of the digger. Their bravery was only to pass me a final message. A final message from the prophet of the substation wall, the vandal who had released me:

THANK YOU!

Lightning Source UK Ltd.
Milton Keynes UK
UKHW020758110222
398547UK00009B/446

9 780244 517601